D1374146

PAULO'S WALL

by *Rachelle DeSimone*

SUMMIT BOOKS

Illustrator: Sue Cornelison

Dedication

For my parents, Gene and Billie Beckman

For information, contact
Perfection Learning® Corporation
1000 North Second Avenue, P.O. Box 500
Logan, Iowa 51546-0500.
Phone: 800-831-4190 • Fax: 800-543-2745
perfectionlearning.com

Paperback ISBN 0-7891-5496-x
Cover Craft® ISBN 0-7569-0859-0
Printed in the U.S.A.

About the Author

Rachelle DeSimone was born and raised in the Los Angeles area. She received a Bachelor's Degree in English Literature and a Master's Degree in Teaching English as a Second Language from California State University in Fullerton. She and her husband have four children: two girls, who were adopted from an orphanage in Russia, and two boys. She teaches reading, journalism, and English to high school students in Whittier, California. *Paulo's Wall* is her first young adult novel.

ONE

I shouldn't have stayed after school to work on the art exhibit. By the time we had finished, I had missed not only the regular bus, but the late bus too. That meant I had to walk home. That was my first mistake.

My second mistake was climbing the fence behind the shopping center and cutting through the alley behind the stores. In my neighborhood, you didn't travel down alleys unless you had backup with you. But I was late, and I knew the shortcut down the alley would get me home a lot faster.

The *cholos* were in the alley. Two of them. I knew them from school. The lumpy-faced one was Spooky. The other one was his homeboy, Loco.

Once I was in the alley, I couldn't retreat. You did that, and the cholos knew you were scared. It's like how dogs sense when an animal or person is afraid. That fear gives the dogs more confidence. So I slowed a bit, hoping the cholos would go on, but they had seen me. They waited, laughing and looking up and down the alley to make sure I was alone.

I kept walking, keeping my head down and making no eye contact. Sometimes this worked, but that day, I think Spooky and his homeboy were bored. They walked toward me. Spooky threw his chest out and did this banty rooster swagger, swinging his arms out and sticking his chin up.

He pushed me to make me stop. "Where you from?"

"Nowhere." I kept my eyes at his feet.

Loco was behind me. He shoved me from the back, knocking me into Spooky.

Spooky pretended to get angry. "What you tryin' to do, *mojado*, push me down?"

I shook my head. I felt Loco pulling at my backpack. He slid it from my shoulders.

"What's this? You a schoolboy?" He shook my backpack and then unzipped it. I had nothing inside but my English notebook and my math book.

Loco swung my pack around and then heaved it into a dumpster. Spooky laughed and waited for me to react. I just stood there, kind of shuffling my feet. I kept my head down until they got bored messing with me and walked on down the alley. Then I pulled my backpack from the dumpster.

I'm a *gallina*—a chicken. I admit it. But doing nothing turned out to be the only smart thing I did that day.

After the gangsters left me in the alley, I hightailed it five blocks until I hit Wilshire Avenue, my street.

I lived on the corner, and there was a wall in front of my house. Nikka, my dog, always waited there for me. The five-foot-high concrete and plaster wall curved around the edge of the property. It really didn't do much as a wall, like keep people in or out. It was more like a marker. When the houses were built here about 30 years ago, the developer had put up the wall and added metal letters painted gold that spelled out "Pleasant Hills."

The funny thing was that there weren't any hills around here. At least not around my neighborhood. Then someone stole the *l* and the *H* so the sign read "P easant ills." Now all the letters were gone, so it was just an ordinary wall that served no purpose. But because it was in front of our house, I thought of it as mine.

That afternoon I could see Nikka sitting under the tree that grew next to the wall. Just the sight of her made me feel calmer.

Nikka turned and ran to me. I knelt and wrapped my arms around her. She wiggled in excitement and licked my face. This greeting was a ritual five days a week, Monday through Friday.

Nikka followed me to the mailbox. I pulled out the few letters and bills. Nothing from Mexico. Mami would be disappointed. She was waiting for a letter from her parents, who live in Durango.

I reached down and rubbed my dog's head. Nikka followed me to the porch and waited patiently while I pulled out the key that I kept on a thin chain around my neck. Nikka followed me inside. I stacked the mail in the basket Mami kept on the bookcase. Nikka's toenails clicked on the hardwood floors Mami scrubbed each week.

I put my backpack on the kitchen counter and wet a sponge. I rubbed at the pack with the sponge, trying to make it look clean. It wasn't too dirty from the dumpster, but I felt better just making sure I had cleaned off the dirt. I'm not a clean freak or anything, but a backpack needs to look decent. At least Loco hadn't dumped my books out into the dumpster.

After I made myself a quesadilla for a snack, I checked the clock. It was time to go to the market for Mami. She never had time since she got home so late, so she left a list and money for me every day. She had written *cumin* on today's list. I circled it so I wouldn't forget.

I liked doing the shopping. It helped my mom. She worked at a warehouse filling orders for soap and perfume. Well, most days I liked shopping, but this day I was a little jumpy because of the cholos. Lately they had been messing with people like me more and more.

I hooked Nikka's leash on to her collar and peered through the window before opening the front door. No one was outside. I listened for any thumpers. Maybe five blocks away I heard the bass from some gangster's car stereo, rhythmic and low. I waited until I could hear the sound change. The thumping was getting harder to hear. Good. The gangsters were moving in the opposite direction. It was safe to go.

It wasn't hard to tell who the gang members were in my neighborhood. They wore a uniform—baggy pants, five sizes larger than what fits. Guys with 30-inch waists wore size 40 pants. They folded the extra material at their waists, then cinched the pants with a belt. The pants hung in folds, thick and creased, hiding skinny legs and making the cholos look bigger than the rest of us.

Of course, their pants were just half of the uniform. They all shaved their heads and wore white T-shirts, perfectly starched and crisp from ironing. I admired their cleanliness, but that's all.

The cholos stole beer from the Fast-Gas, spray-painted graffiti on the bus stop benches, and etched their names into the windows of Medina's Used Appliance Store. They stood in a group at the Gardens apartment house, occasionally flashing signs made with their fingers at passing cars.

If someone new drove into our neighborhood, the older boys would surround the car, pulling up their T-shirts to show bright tattoos on their chests or shoulders, informing the newcomer whose territory he was entering.

White people used to live here, but when the Latino families from East L.A. started moving in, the white families disappeared. We had one Chinese guy who lived a block over. He knew Spanish, though, and didn't bug anyone. This Russian immigrant family had moved in last year but got out of the neighborhood in record time. And the blacks, they didn't come around. There was some bad blood between them and the cholos.

It used to be that if you were brown, you were okay—you were part of the barrio. But then things became different, unfortunately for me. To be a homeboy, you *really* had to be a homeboy—a gangster—and I wasn't. Just being brown used to keep me safe, but not anymore.

TWO

I locked my front door and stuck the key inside my shirt. Nikka was so excited, she was jumping. She loved to walk. Bargain Barn was close, three blocks, and the walk was never enough for Nikka.

As I walked, Nikka sniffed everything. Cars filled the driveway of Heriberto Gonzalez's house next door. Fenders, hoods, radiators, and rims were littered on the lawn and stacked up against the garage. That day a truck with its hood up blocked the driveway. As we passed the house, Nikka stopped to sniff at a set of legs underneath the truck. Heriberto slid out.

"Hey, Paulo," he said, waving his black hand. Nikka sniffed his oily hand and backed away.

"Market?"

"Yeah," I said.

"Mom working?"

"Yeah."

"Dog okay?"

"Yeah."

"School okay?"

"Yeah. Truck fixed?"

"Nah, not yet."

Heriberto and I never talked in full sentences, but we talked every day. Mom told me when I was younger that if I ever had problems before she got home, I was to go to Heriberto for help. Heriberto is always at home working on somebody's car.

It was nice having a backup person if there was ever trouble, but I was usually okay by myself. I'd been letting myself in the house after school since I was eight years old.

Nikka and I walked by Fernando Estrada's house. The Estradas had two dogs, and Nikka enjoyed visiting them. Concho and Osa raced to the fence when they spotted Nikka. Nikka strained at her leash. Osa's pregnant belly was big. Fernando told me that I could come to see the puppies when they were born.

I waited while Nikka sniffed and whined at the chain-link fence. I liked imagining what Nikka, Concho, and Osa talked about when they met. I figured they probably talked about food or about the rooster in Antonio Garcia's backyard that woke everyone up at daybreak. Dogs have simple lives, but that's good. I wouldn't mind such a simple life myself.

Paulo's Wall

I gave a slight pull on the leash to let Nikka know it was time to go. Nikka followed, stepping around the oil on the asphalt just as I had.

At the market, I tied Nikka to the bike rack. "Stay, girl," I said, although it wasn't necessary. Nikka wouldn't try to free herself. She would sit patiently and wait for me to return.

I picked up milk, *masa* for the tamales Mami makes, tortillas, cumin, a whole chicken, and a box of cereal. I checked off each item as I went and added the price next to it on the list. I had to stay in our budget. My first time shopping I had gone over the amount my mother had given me, so I had to put things back. A girl waiting behind me in line had laughed, and the others in line had been impatient. Now I made sure to add when I put anything in the cart.

I also had to consider how much weight I would be carrying. I looked at the load in the cart, added a ten-pound bag of dog food, and went to the register.

I had trained Nikka to help carry the groceries. I would tie one of the plastic bags filled with a few items to her collar. Because she had long legs, the bag didn't touch the ground as long as I tied it up high enough on the halter collar.

Isabel, the cashier, smiled when she saw me.

Her shaved-off eyebrows were penciled in with black, and when she smiled, they moved up high on her forehead. When I talked to her, I could never keep my eyes on anything but her eyebrows. I guess that's better than looking at her chest. Sometimes I find my eyes going in that direction with girls at school when we talk. Then I get all embarrassed when I realize where my eyes have been, and I wonder if the girl knew where I was looking. I wish I could just keep my eyes on safe places.

"How's Nikka?" Isabel asked.

I pointed outside. "Fine. Waiting for me, as usual."

"If you ever want to sell that dog . . ."

"I know . . . give you first chance."

The first time Isabel had said she wanted to buy Nikka, I was furious. How dare she think I would even consider selling my dog? But now I knew it was Isabel's way of saying she liked Nikka.

I gave Isabel the money and said good-bye. Nikka was watching for me and gave a bark when I approached. I tied a bag to her collar. She walked like a soldier in a parade. I liked her energy. She never seemed to tire.

At the corner a thumper drove by. I moved behind a car parked by the muffler shop. Nikka waited. She knew the drill. I checked out the car that cruised by. It was a lowered gray Honda with tinted windows and chrome caps. The car slowed a bit but passed. Safe.

My friend Manuel always said I was paranoid about drive-bys. Maybe I was. But I had been on the street a couple of times when guys flashed guns as they drove by. I hated that.

When we got closer to home, Nikka sped up. She knew I would give her a reward from the refrigerator—a hunk of cheese or a bite of meat.

I opened the door, and Nikka ran in ahead of me.

After I put the groceries away and gave Nikka a treat and fresh water, I flipped on the TV and sat down to brush Nikka's coat. Mami allowed Nikka inside the front room as long as I vacuumed the rug to pick up dog hairs. Nikka's brown coat was thick and long. She loved to be brushed. She lay on the carpet, her long legs sprawled out and her head resting on my feet.

I kept my homework on the couch beside me. During the commercials, I answered some of the questions for social studies. I usually saved my math homework for later in the evening. I needed to concentrate on the math problems, and the TV distracted me.

Besides, my mother didn't allow me to

watch TV much in the evening. She hated most of the TV shows that I liked. I loved the reruns of "Married with Children." She hated Al Bundy. I don't know why. Maybe because he likes to watch TV and sit on the couch with his hand tucked in his pants. Hey, he's comfortable.

I kept the blinds on the front window slightly open so I could see when my mom arrived. From my seat on the couch, I had a view of everyone who approached.

Nikka had just closed her eyes and I was changing the channel on the TV from one talk show to another when I saw two shaved heads. Cholos. I recognized them right away.

The one in front was definitely Loco, the one who had taken my backpack. And there was Spooky, his homeboy.

They approached the wall in front of my house, checking up and down the street. Nobody else was outside. Behind the gangsters, the sky was dark with tinges of red and gold, the end of a September sunset. The street was quiet except for the hum of air conditioners from the apartment house.

Spooky pulled a can of spray paint from his pants. He sprayed the wall while Loco looked for police. Now it was Loco's turn to spray the wall while Spooky kept watch.

My skin felt tight, and I gripped the remote until my fingers hurt.

That was my wall.

Spooky capped the spray paint can, and the can disappeared back into his pants. The boys moved away quickly, looking up and down the street as they walked. When they were gone, I went outside and walked to the front of the wall to read the writing. "Tres Palmas Spooky y Loco"—the name of their gang and their nicknames. The black, spindly writing reminded me of spiders, long-legged spiders, crawling all over the wall.

I knew what the graffiti meant. The gang was claiming my neighborhood, my street, and my wall.

THREE

I stared at the wall for a few minutes. Should I just leave the writing? I imagined my mother's face when she saw it. She was really afraid of cholos. Her best friend, Lilian, had a brother who was killed in a drive-by shooting in Norwalk. Mami would be really freaked if she saw the graffiti on our wall.

I went back inside. Nikka followed me.

For some strange reason, the graffiti made me see with fresh eyes. Our neighborhood was looking ratty, I admit it. Mami said it hadn't been so bad when she and Papi moved in 17 years ago. Back then, people had kept their houses painted nice and watered their lawns more.

Now, the houses were fading, and the bushes and trees were overgrown. The city needed to repave the street, and the sidewalks were a mess because the roots of the trees had pushed the cement up in different places.

But Mami said we should be happy we didn't have to live in an apartment. I was. I couldn't have kept Nikka if we lived in an apartment. Our house had a small backyard, big enough for Nikka to run in and chase the Frisbee that I threw for her.

A backyard was important for Mami too, so she could raise her vegetables and her two chickens. Collecting the eggs, she said, reminded her of Mexico. Before she immigrated to the United States, Mami had lived on a farm with her eight brothers and sisters and her mother and father.

When she was 16, her father sent her to California to make money for the family. Her father hadn't been able to make enough to keep everyone fed. Even now, 17 years later, Mami sent money home to her parents every month.

I couldn't do that. I'd be too tempted to spend the money. But Mami was disciplined about it. She said she owed it to her parents for taking care of her when she was little. She wanted to help her younger brothers and sisters too. Mami was the oldest. She didn't even know two of her sisters. They had been born after she came to the United States. One of her sisters, *mi tía* Rubi, was 13, one year younger than I am! Strange, huh? I've never met Aunt Rubi, but if I did, I'd just call her Rubi. It'd be too weird to call her "aunt."

I went out the back door. The two chickens

were squabbling over melon seeds they had discovered by the back steps. Nikka ignored the chickens and followed me. She sat and waited while I swung open the aluminum door of the garage. I flipped on a light and found some paint.

It was my uncle's paint, but I knew *Tío* Miguel wouldn't mind. Tío Miguel lived in an apartment and stored his equipment in our garage. Since my mother didn't have a car, we had plenty of room for Miguel's tools. Miguel had most of his tools on shelves, but I had to thread my way through the boxes and tires he had stacked on the floor to get to the paint.

I carried everything to the front of the house. Last year, I had helped Mami paint the kitchen, so I knew what I needed to do. I poured paint into the pan and dipped the roller. I allowed the excess to drip off the brush into the pan, and then I rolled white paint over the black letters. I had to roll many times until the graffiti disappeared. Nikka sat beside me, watching with her usual patience.

When Nikka had first come to live with us, she chewed everything in sight. Whenever I opened the door to the backyard, Nikka would jump on me. That was annoying, especially a couple of times when Nikka had had dirty paws and had gotten mud all over my jeans. It had taken a year before she settled down. Mami had said that she would get calmer once she was no longer a puppy. She was right. Nikka didn't jump on us anymore, and she didn't chew anything but the bones we threw to her after Mami made *carnitas*.

Nikka was a friendly dog too. She'd gotten used to the chickens and didn't chase them around the yard like she had when she was younger. That afternoon she waited right beside me until I had finished painting the wall and cleaned the roller brush and pan.

That evening when Mami got home, it was dark, so she didn't notice the fresh paint on the wall. She greeted me with a hug and a tired, "Hi, *m'ijo*."

I watched her as we ate dinner together. I wondered if I should tell her about the graffiti. It would be another worry for her. Mami was getting older, I realized. Her thick black hair had some gray streaks. Just that week, Mami had stood in front of the mirror parting her hair and counting the gray strands she saw. And Tío Miguel had teased her and called her an old lady when he saw the gray. Mami didn't laugh then, although she usually laughed at most of Miguel's teasing.

When I stood next to my mother, I was at least five inches taller. Mami was a small woman. She stood 5'2" and weighed 105 pounds. I was glad I was built like my father. Papi had been tall with big shoulders. When I was younger, my father had carried me on his shoulders everywhere, especially at the swap meets.

I remembered the view; I had been able to look down the aisles and see the tables of clothing, cookware, baskets, jewelry, and toys for sale. Each vendor got a 20- by 20-foot square of pavement to display stuff. From Papi's shoulders, it looked like a patchwork quilt with each square a different color and texture. The most colorful squares were the ones where vendors sold fruit—screaming-yellow bananas, rich green watermelon, golden red papaya, burgundy grapes, and fuzzy Australian kiwi. The smell of sweet fruit from the produce vendors still reminded me of Papi and the swap meets.

Papi had taken me to the swap meets every Saturday. He looked for old lawn mowers there. He would buy them, fix them, spray them with black enamel, and then sell them to the Mexican gardeners who worked uptown where the homes were big and the owners didn't do their own yard work.

But fixing lawn mowers had been Papi's side

job. During the week, he had worked at Esco Metal. He helped transport pipes and metal plates. He liked the job, Mami said. Everyone spoke Spanish, even the foreman, and the workers had paid holidays.

Papi named me after himself, Pablo. Papi's father, my grandfather, had been a Pablo too. Mami said she and Papi gave me the name Paulo, a variation of Pablo, because it would get too confusing with three Pablos.

Papi died from cancer when I was seven. Mami wore her hair up for months. At night I could hear her crying. Now she didn't cry. She didn't talk about Papi much anymore either. But we kept a photograph of Papi in a gold frame that was slowly turning a turtle brown in our dining room on the chest where Mami kept the tablecloths. When I was younger, I liked to think that Papi was eating with us. Once, when I was eight, I had put a third plate with rice and beans on it in front of the photograph, but Mami had started crying. I never did that again.

Mami cleared her plate from the table while I was still eating. She called to me from the kitchen, "Don't forget that Saturday we go to Yvette's *quincenera*. You'll need your best shirt and pants."

I hadn't forgotten. I was looking forward to

the party. Yvette was the daughter of Lilian, Mami's friend. Even though Yvette was a sophomore, a grade higher in school than me, she had always been nice to me. I wouldn't be 15 until August. Some girls didn't like talking to younger boys, but Yvette wasn't like that. Maybe she would even dance with me at the party.

The next day at school, I told my best friend Manuel about the graffiti. I'd known Manuel for eight years. We had both been placed in an English-as-a-Second-Language class in second grade. The teacher had put us at the same table.

Manuel had looked me up and down. "You look like me," he had said in Spanish.

I had stared at his brown skin, his broad nose, and thick black hair. "You look like me."

"Maybe we're brothers."

"No, just look-alikes," I'd said. We had been friends since. I had grown taller than Manuel by fourth grade, but we still looked the same. My hair was straighter than Manuel's, but we usually had the same long haircut. We kept it long because the gangsters wore theirs short, usually shaved. No way did I want anybody to mistake me for a cholo. A guy could get shot for having hair too short. Today, Manuel's hair fell over his right eye.

Manuel shook his head to flip his hair back.

"Bad news. You know the gangsters will come back. They're marking their territory, like dogs do. Disgusting."

"I know. I see their name, Tres Palmas, all over the streets by my house. It's even on the telephone poles."

Manuel nodded. "It's worse when another gang crosses out the name and writes in their own. That means you're in the middle of a war or a drive-by."

I nodded. "I guess it could be worse. But it's my wall they're tagging."

"Remember when someone tagged my locker last year?" Manuel said. "I was glad when the custodians repainted all the lockers so mine looked like everyone else's. Who are the gangsters? Do you know them?"

"They're guys in my neighborhood. Albert's brother is one of them," I said.

"Albert? The guy in our social studies class?"

"Yes, that Albert. It's his brother, Spooky, and his homeboy, Loco. Spooky's a sophomore or junior, but I don't ever see him at school. "

"He's probably been kicked out," said Manuel.

After school, I watched Manuel climb into his brother's car. Manuel didn't have to take the bus like I did. He usually got a ride home, but if he didn't, he could walk. His house was less than a mile from school.

Sometimes I wished Manuel could come to my house, but Manuel's mother didn't allow him to go to my neighborhood. She said it was dangerous.

I took the bus home. I hated how the kids pushed. And sometimes the bus was so crowded, we had to sit three in a seat. A bunch of the kids had complained to the school that we needed more buses, but the principal said there wasn't enough money. So we sat elbow-to-elbow, shoulder-to-shoulder, scrunching together like rats in a cage.

Sometimes it was so loud from people yelling and screaming that the bus driver had to pull over and ask us to be quiet. It would be quiet for a few minutes, but then it became louder than ever. Before the end of the route, some guys in the back usually started throwing paper. The bus driver had to pull over again, and we would wait until things quieted down again. Being a bus driver has to be the worst job in the world.

That afternoon I sat by a girl I knew from art class, but we didn't speak. She pretended to be doing her homework. I stared out of the window. I wished I could get her to talk, but when I was around girls, I felt like Heriberto. Words just didn't flow out of my mouth. The only girl I'd ever been able to talk to was Yvette. I wondered how her party would be.

I was glad when my bus stop came. I checked for Nikka. There she was, at the wall.

And the wall—it was written on again with black spray paint. The graffiti was back.

FOUR

THIS time Spooky and Loco had spray-painted "Tres Palmas" in bigger letters. The entire wall was covered.

I clenched my hands. My skin burned as if I'd been spray-painted. It's just a wall, I told myself. It's just a stupid wall. While I stood gazing at the wall, Nikka whined and tried to lick my hand. I relaxed my fist.

"Hello, girl. Sorry I didn't say hello right away," I said, rubbing Nikka's shoulders and patting her back.

I decided to eat something before I painted the wall. I needed energy to do the wall this time. I would have to repaint the entire thing.

It took me nearly an hour to roll over all the letters. After I cleaned up, I walked to Heriberto's house.

Heriberto had climbed under the hood of a car, but he stuck his head out when he heard me call his name.

"Graffiti on the wall."

"Saw it."

"I painted over it."

"Saw it."

"Today—it's there again."

"Stupid cholos."

"Yeah."

"Don't mess with 'em."

"Yeah."

Heriberto disappeared into the car, and I walked home with Nikka.

The next afternoon, the graffiti was there again.

And the next. And the next.

Each time I had to paint over the mess before Mami got home.

"I'm getting tired of painting over their graffiti. And I'm running out of paint," I told Manuel.

"I think we got some old paint in our carport," Manuel said. "I could ask my dad if you can have it."

"Thanks. I hope I won't need it. Don't you think they'll get tired of tagging the wall eventually?"

Manuel nodded. "Sure. Sure they will."

"I'd better take your dad's paint, just in case."

That afternoon, I waited and watched,

hidden from street view on the porch. I carried Nikka's brush outside and spent the time brushing her.

It was almost dark. The sun, combined with the haze of smog, made a red glow in the sky. Nikka had just about fallen asleep when we both heard voices. Nikka sat up, but I put my hand on her head to make her stay. I peered over the top of the porch wall. Gangbangers.

I took a second look. I couldn't tell who the gangsters were, but they were right in front of the wall, and I heard the *ping-ping-ping* of a paint can being shaken.

I walked to the middle of the lawn. From where I stood, the gangsters were out of sight, but I could hear their voices and the *psssssssssss* of paint shooting out of a can.

"Stop it. Don't tag my wall, you jerks!" I yelled.

Two figures stepped from behind the wall. Spooky and Loco. They just stared at me for a few seconds. Then Spooky laughed. He motioned to Loco, and they both started walking toward me. I saw Spooky pull a flashlight out of his big pocket. A heavy flashlight. To hit me with.

I backed up, my hand going to my neck to locate the house key. I walked backward as quickly as I could, but my legs seemed stiff and heavy. I took about ten steps, and then I realized I wouldn't make it to the porch. They were coming fast.

Suddenly Nikka was there, in front, growling and showing her fantastic white teeth. The hair on her back was up in a tall ridge, and her tail stood straight and stiff.

Spooky and Loco stopped. Nikka took a step forward. They took a few steps backward. Then they turned and walked back to the street. Nikka kept growling and advancing until they had walked to the sidewalk across the street.

Once on the sidewalk, Loco and Spooky slowed down. Loco called to me, his arms jerking and his fingers pointing, "You can't dis us and live. We're gonna send you back to Mexico in a box, Wall-boy."

Nikka stayed next to me watching the two until they were out of sight. Her body relaxed, and I sat beside her, resting my arms on my knees. I had never before seen Nikka like that. She had reminded me of a wolf, and now, in a second, I understood how dogs are related to wilder animals.

What would have happened if Nikka hadn't been there? Why had I been so stupid? Like a good *gallina*, I should have stayed inside. Now

Loco and Spooky would come hunting for me.

I hurried back inside and then remembered I needed to paint over the graffiti. My hands shook a little as I worked in the dark. I kept checking behind me, watching my back. I knew Nikka would warn me if someone approached, but I still hurried to complete the job. I just had time to wash up before Mami arrived home. It was dark when she got off the bus, so she didn't notice the fresh paint on the wall. I was glad. I helped her get dinner ready. She was tired because she had worked overtime.

"We're both exhausted, aren't we, *m'ijo*," she said as we ate dinner silently. I nodded. Under the dining room light, Mami looked older. Around her eyes were wrinkles I had never noticed before. She worked too hard taking care of me. And she worried about stuff, like paying the rent, having enough money for my school clothes, and not having health insurance. No way was I going to tell her about Spooky and Loco.

Spooky and Loco didn't spray the wall the next day. I was hoping it was all over. I told Manuel that maybe, because of Nikka, the cholos would back off.

"You're dreaming," Manuel said. "They won't give up that easy. The more turf they can claim as their own, the more powerful they feel.

They're gonna fight for your street."

Manuel was right. When I came home from school that Friday, I saw the wall was covered from top to bottom with graffiti, not only with the names of Spooky and Loco, but all the others in the Tres Palmas gang. And there, in the middle, was my name—*Paulo*—in big letters with an X through it.

FIVE

I called Manuel. Usually we didn't talk on the phone. Once we said good-bye at school, we wouldn't talk until class the next day. And we rarely talked on the weekends.

So Manuel knew something was up.

"What's going on?"

"My name's X-ed out. On the wall."

"How'd they know your name?"

"I don't know," I said, winding the phone cord around my wrist so tight it hurt. "Maybe Albert told them. Maybe they asked around the neighborhood."

"That's bad. They're gonna hurt you now. That's what the X means, you know."

"Of course. What should I do?"

"Don't you dare X over their names. They take that seriously."

"I know. But I am going to paint over the whole thing. Again."

"Why don't you just leave it? Let them think they own the neighborhood."

"And let my mom see my name with an *X* through it? No way."

I hung up and got out my paint supplies. I was actually getting faster at painting, and neater, I noticed, as I wiped a run before it dripped on the street. Maybe I could get a job painting for a living. Then someday I'd thank Loco and Spooky for teaching me a trade.

Nikka seemed bored. This routine by the wall was no fun for her, I knew. When I had finished, I took her into the backyard and threw the Frisbee. She leaped about two feet into the air and twisted her head to catch it. Years ago, when she first caught a Frisbee, I had been so excited. I knew dogs could retrieve balls and sticks, but to catch things—that's pretty good.

Actually, Nikka was a better athlete than many humans. She was a better one than I was, that's for sure. Underneath their fur, dogs have intensely defined muscles, some dogs more than others, of course.

Like pit bulls. I know some people hate them. Mami did. I take that back. She hated their owners. She thought people who owned pit bulls wanted to pretend how powerful and mean they were by having powerful, mean dogs.

Some pit bulls are mean. But their muscles are beautiful. Their necks are solid ridges of power. There was an old Armenian man at the swap meets who brought his pit bull named Bull every Saturday to guard his stuff when he had to use the restroom. The man sold knock-off brand name sunglasses; he pretended they were hot so people would buy them. You know, winking at the customer and saying, "They fell off a truck." Anyway, when the old guy would leave his booth, no one messed with his sunglasses because of his pit bull.

Bull was actually friendly to people he knew. The old man had let me pet Bull once. Bull's muscles were unbelievable, almost as rigid as the security bars over my bedroom windows. You could touch the strength. No lie.

Nikka wasn't like a pit bull. Her muscles were hidden behind her fur, but she was strong. I could feel her strength when we wrestled. She was always careful not to bite me, but she would grab on to me, and I could feel the power in her jaws.

I wondered what it would be like to have that kind of power. I decided that I'd ask for a weight set for my birthday. Maybe Tío Miguel and Mami could go in together on a gift and get me a bench press. I'd start working out and building up my upper body first. Girls might talk to me if I had a buff body. Besides, I was gonna need muscles if I had more problems with cholos.

Paulo's Wall

That Saturday was Yvette's *quincenera*. I found my black pants and white shirt at the back of my closet. Mami looked good in her yellow dress with the short sleeves. She was still pretty, even though she was getting gray. Once I asked her why she hadn't remarried after Papi died. She said she had never found another man like Papi. That made me feel good, like my father was extra-special or something.

Yvette looked pretty, too, in her white dress at church. Her brown hair was up, except for some pieces of hair that curled around her neck. She had on makeup and thick lipstick. I had never seen her like that. She looked great, don't get me wrong, but so much older. There was no way I could talk to her—not with her looking that old and that good.

She had six *chambeláns*. They were wearing matching tuxedos. I wondered if one of the escorts was her boyfriend. Mami had said two of the chambeláns were Yvette's cousins and the others were friends.

The priest, Father Edgar, spoke really beautiful Spanish. Mami said he had been born and raised in Spain. I hadn't heard Spanish like that before. I told Mami his Spanish sounded different.

"Yes," Mami said. "To me, it's elegant, like

thin silver icing on a white cake."

I had never thought about language being beautiful or elegant before. I sat back and just listened to Father Edgar talking without really paying attention to his words. It was cool.

Yvette gave a short, nervous speech using the microphone. She thanked her parents, her godparents, her cousins, aunts, uncles—everyone. Then she placed her bouquet of flowers on the altar of the shrine for the Virgin Mary.

After the church service, we left for the party. Her family had rented a big hall at the Girls and Boys Club in Uptown. They arrived in a limousine. Yvette got out holding the front of her white dress.

I tried to catch her eye, but she was too busy greeting people and being hugged and kissed. I put her present on a long table where a pile of wrapped gifts sat. Mami had bought her a basket of soaps, really pretty ones that smelled good, and glass bottles of bath oil with colored flowers inside. Girls like that kind of thing.

Mami was supposed to help get the buffet table set up. She disappeared into the kitchen. I didn't know anyone there. Yvette went to Victory High School. Most of the kids at the quincenera were from that school.

After the buffet was set up, everyone got plates and stood in line for food. Yvette spent her time talking to guests. She didn't seem to have time to enjoy anything. She couldn't even sit down to eat. Her mother, Lilian, was busy too. I guess hosting a party is hard work.

Mami and I sat together at a table with some people we didn't know. Mami started talking to the lady next to her. She had a daughter, Delia, who was a senior at Victory High. At first I thought Delia wouldn't want to talk to a freshman, but she was friendly. She told me that she was going to cosmetology school after she graduated because she wanted to cut hair and do nails in a salon.

"Do you know what you want to do after you finish school?" she asked.

I shook my head. I had no idea. I told her I liked animals. Maybe I would do something with animals. Or cars.

Delia asked me how I knew Yvette. I told her that Yvette's mom and my mother were friends from work.

"Yvette and I just got to be friends last year," Delia said. "We were in the same P.E. class. I was the only junior in the class. I failed P.E. my freshman year."

She laughed at my expression. "Yeah, I

know. It's pretty hard to fail P.E. You have to work at your F.

"Anyway, Yvette and I were being hassled by some hoochies in class. One girl said we were talking to her boyfriend. Two of the hoochies caught Yvette alone in the locker room and started punching her and pulling her hair."

Yvette fighting hoochies—it was hard to imagine.

"I came in and pulled one hoochie away from her so at least it'd be a fair fight, but before I could do anything, a P.E. teacher stopped the fight."

"Was Yvette hurt?"

"Not too bad. Just a black eye. And some of her hair got pulled out."

"What happened to the other girls?"

"It was their second fight that year. They got kicked out of school."

All evening I thought about what Delia had told me. So I wasn't the only one with problems like that.

When I finally got a chance to dance with Yvette, I didn't mention the fight. Actually, Yvette asked *me* to dance. She had come to my table, talked a minute with Mami, and then turned to me and said, "Hey, don't just sit there like a dead fish. You gotta dance at my party."

I was glad it had happened that way. We danced to a salsa song that was so loud we couldn't talk. That was fine with me. I wasn't sure if I could move my mouth and my body at the same time anyway. And when the song ended, some older guy was waiting to dance with her. So I never really talked to her. She waved to me as she moved on.

It was a good quincenera. Mami even danced. That was strange. I hadn't seen her dance before. This man named Edgar from her work asked her. He talked to her a long time too. Mami laughed as much as she does when she watches a Cantinflas movie. Cantinflas was this old funny actor in Mexican movies. Mami thought his movies were the funniest ever, so Edgar must have been funny to rate up there with Cantinflas.

The only bad thing happened after the quincenera. Edgar walked Mami out to Lilian's car. I followed, trying not to listen to their conversation. Edgar was asking Mami something about the next weekend—dinner at a restaurant called El Cielo. Edgar said in Spanish, "The music is excellent."

We heard cars racing up the street. One was a fixed-up Honda with tinted windows and oversized tires. Another was a big American car.

The two cars were fighting. Really, the drivers were fighting and using their cars as weapons. The Honda cut off the bigger American car, and that car hit the streetlight at the corner. Edgar and Mami started to go to the accident, but then the people inside the car started climbing out of the windows. They were gangsters. They didn't wait for the police or anyone. They took off running, all in different directions, about five of them. There were no police to catch them anyway. The police didn't come until about ten minutes later. Then Edgar heard one of them say that the wrecked car had been reported stolen from Hacienda Heights the day before.

People from different buildings gathered around for a few minutes, but left when they realized nobody had been hurt and we were just staring at a bashed-up piece of metal.

Nobody wanted to talk to the police, even when the police asked if anyone in the crowd had seen the accident. I remained silent. Mami and Edgar didn't say anything either. Mami and I were legal, me especially since I was born here, but still, you just didn't talk to police. Period. I knew police weren't the same as INS officers, but they were related, and my people just didn't talk to people wearing uniforms.

SIX

THAT Monday after school, I told Manuel about the quincenera. He walked with me to the school gate. I was telling him about Delia and how, even though she was a senior, she had talked with me and even danced once with me.

"Cool. So you're finally talking to girls," Manuel said. "I was getting worried."

Manuel can joke about it because he's already had a girlfriend. For about five months in eighth grade, Manuel and this girl, Leticia, met at her locker between classes. Then Manuel would walk her home, and he'd call her twice every evening. In March she'd moved back to Mexico. Manuel had been sad for weeks.

I told Manuel about the car accident we saw after the quincenera. I told him how the gangsters had all run in different directions, all five of them.

"Do they plan that?" I asked Manuel. "Do they say, 'If we ever get into trouble, run, but run in different directions to make it harder for police to catch us'?"

Manuel laughed. "No, their minds just work differently than ours. You know how you can turn on the light in the kitchen and a mess of cockroaches will run every which way and you end up only being able to squish one?"

"That's it. Cockroach mentality."

As we were talking, a car pulled up to the curb. Manuel nudged me. "Albert's getting into that car."

I stared. The older boys in the car stared back. Then I recognized one of the shaved heads. It was Spooky. Spooky of Tres Palmas. And Spooky recognized me. He was getting out of the car.

I didn't wait for the car door to open completely. I took off running up the steps. Manuel ran with me. We looked for an open classroom door. Mr. Shagallini was cleaning up the art room when Manuel and I skidded in.

"Hello. What are you two doing?" Mr. Shagallini said, stopping to look at us.

Manuel looked behind but no one was following us. "We were wondering if you needed any help cleaning up. Paulo's taking the late bus, so we thought we'd find something to do."

Despite my nervousness, I couldn't help appreciating Manuel's quick thinking. I didn't mind either scrubbing the art tables or taking the late bus home that afternoon.

Mr. Shagallini thanked us. "Anytime you need to take the late bus, you can come to my classroom, boys, and help out," he said, taking the dirty rags and cleanser from us.

I nodded. Later I said to Manuel, "I hope I don't have to spend any more afternoons cleaning for Shagallini, but with Tres Palmas after me, who knows what I'm gonna have to do?"

"You mean, to keep alive?"

"Yeah, but you don't have to actually say it that way—like I could die," I said, pushing Manuel with my elbow.

Manuel laughed. "I'm not planning your funeral or anything like that. But have you checked out Memorial Hills Cemetery? You know, people are dying to get in there."

"A stupid joke, dope. Knock it off." I was glad the bus was parked in the loading zone so I could say good-bye to Manuel.

Nikka was anxiously waiting for me by the wall. I didn't stop to greet her. Once off the bus, I ran for the house, my key ready. Nikka sprinted after me. I locked the door behind us and peered out of the window. No one was there. I was safe, for today.

I stayed inside the entire afternoon. I kept hearing thumpers driving down my street. Maybe it was my imagination, but they seemed to slow down by my house. The vibration of the heavy bass of the music traveled through the walls and hurt my ears. Nikka whined each time a thumper went by.

That evening, Mami was puzzled, I knew, that I hadn't done the shopping. She had planned to make carnitas, but I hadn't bought the meat. I helped her make bean tostadas instead.

As we were eating, Mami watched me. "Are you feeling okay, m'ijo?"

"I'm fine. Just tired today like I told you."

I took a few bites before I spoke again. "Do you think we can rent some other house—in another neighborhood, Mami?"

Mami's eyes widened. "You know why we live here. We can't afford higher rent."

I nodded. I struggled to take another bite of the tostada.

That evening, Nikka lay next to my bed, and I dropped my hand over the side and petted her. It seemed forever until I felt tired enough to sleep. Nikka sensed my mood and whined softly as I flopped about in bed.

"We're in trouble, Nikka. Big trouble," I whispered.

The next morning I ate my breakfast without tasting a thing. Mami said good-bye, but I didn't hear her. She tapped me on the shoulder and repeated herself.

"Oh, good-bye, Mami."

"Are you okay?"

I forced a smile. "Sure, Mami, see you later."

After my mother left, I finished dressing and made sure my key was around my neck on the chain. I gave Nikka fresh water and said good-bye to her.

I almost opened the door, but something made me check the window first. There, standing outside by the wall, were Spooky, Loco, and four other cholos. They all wore the uniform—oversized, baggy pants, hung low on the hip and kept up with canvas belts. The gangsters wore flannel Pendletons, part of their fall and winter uniform, neatly pressed and matching in color with their pants.

The group laughed and talked and kept looking toward the house. One, a guy I'd never seen before, took out a knife and began scratching something into the bark of the tree near the wall.

I heard the bus approaching. I was supposed to be outside waiting at the stop, but I couldn't leave, not with six of Tres Palmas waiting to jump me. As the bus pulled to the stop, the gangbangers turned and looked at my house, expecting me to appear.

They know where I live. They know I ride the bus, I thought. My stomach twisted. What else do they know about me?

After the bus drove off, the boys waited for a few more minutes. Finally, with a shrug, Spooky motioned the others to follow him. They left, ambling down the street, smoking cigarettes and talking.

SEVEN

I had missed the bus. Now I would have to walk the three miles to school. I grabbed my books and looked out the window again. The boys were nowhere in sight.

I opened the door and slid outside. I waited by the door, but no one stepped out of the bushes from behind any houses.

I took off running. I needed to run five blocks until I was out of Tres Palmas territory. I moved through the neighborhood at a pace that would have impressed my P.E. teacher. I didn't stop to talk to Heriberto who was working on a black Camaro in the driveway. I barely waved to Antonio Garcia who was watering the vegetables he grew in a long strip of land next to his garage. I ignored Concho and Osa even though they barked at the fence as I ran by.

The only problem was that after those five blocks, I would be in Brown Brothers territory. Then, after that, I had to run through Barrio Loco territory. Once I got a mile or so from school, I was safe. No gangs claimed the neighborhoods around La Vista High School. White families with money lived there. Occasionally some rich white punks in black clothing vandalized the area, but they were too busy listening to their music, smoking weed, and fighting with their parents to do much damage to anybody else.

I had missed first period entirely and was late to second period. Manuel looked up at me as I came in.

"What happened?"

"I'll tell you later," I said, noticing that Albert, Spooky's brother, was looking at me.

At lunch, Manuel listened without eating his tomato sandwich. When I finished, he shook his head sadly.

"They're like wolves, you know, hunting in groups. They'll get you when you're alone."

"You're supposed to make me feel better, not worse. Isn't that what best friends do?" I said, irritated.

"How can I make you feel better? I'm just telling you the truth."

We ate in silence.

Manuel finally spoke. "You need a plan of action."

"Like what?"

"I don't know, Paulo. If I did, I'd tell you. You know that."

I walked back to class thinking about what Manuel had said. I did need a plan of action or at least some way of defending myself.

That evening, Tío Miguel came over for dinner. Mami prepared rice and chicken fajitas with guacamole, Miguel's favorite meal.

While Mami was working in the kitchen, Miguel sat watching television and petting Nikka. I liked how my uncle looked. He had a dark mustache, and he was buff. Miguel worked out with weights, and it showed. He was not very tall; in fact, people might say he was short, but he looked tough.

Miguel had followed Mami to the United States when he turned 16. Mami had gotten him a job as a painter, and at night Miguel went to adult school for English classes. Miguel's English was now almost perfect, although he had an accent that he said he probably could never get rid of.

Miguel loved living in the United States. He told me he was not going to live in Mexico ever again. He would visit, but his home was now the United States.

"Why?" I had asked.

"I can make a lot of money here. And life is

so much better. In Mexico, I would have to work for 15 years before I could buy a truck like I have now."

Miguel's Chevy Suburban was pale green with chrome hubcaps. The truck had tinted electric windows and rear air-conditioning. Miguel had an awesome sound system in the Suburban. He blared his ranchero music from the speakers mounted in the back. Sometimes I had to shout when I was riding in the truck. Mami got mad at Miguel because she said he was gonna go deaf if he listened to his music that loud. So he always turned it down when she was in the truck.

Miguel spent every weekend polishing the Suburban. I loved it when he took me on errands in it. Now he was saving his money to buy a trailer and jet ski. He said he would take me to Lake Mead when he got the ski. I knew it would take him some time to save enough for both the trailer and jet ski because he sent money to his parents in Mexico every month, just like Mami did.

When Miguel and Mami got together, they talked about their brothers and sisters, all strangers to me. I knew Mami and Miguel missed their family, but I was bored when they talked about people I'd never met. It bugged me, too, because it was as if they were part of this other world that I didn't know.

In my Spanish for Native Speakers class, Señora Lopez showed us slides of her trips to Mexico. She drove through Durango once and showed us pictures of that area when we were studying the different states. I thought, Hm . . . so this is where Mami and Miguel are from. It didn't look too exciting. But it looked safe.

I wondered how my life would be different if I had grown up in Durango. I wouldn't know English. I would probably have to work on the farm. Maybe I wouldn't be in school. Mami said that in Durango many boys are needed in the fields to work, so they don't go to school after sixth grade.

I was actually glad I got to go to school. As boring as my classes were sometimes, I'd rather be there than picking strawberries in a hot field. That's what my cousins did in Durango.

Tonight, Miguel watched TV and patted Nikka. I waited until a commercial before I asked the question I had been holding inside ever since Miguel had arrived.

"Tío Miguel, how does a guy defend himself? I mean, if someone tried to get you, what would you do?"

Miguel stood up. "You want to learn some moves?"

"Yes," I said, glad that he understood.

Miguel showed me some punches. He showed me how to jab with my closed fist and protect myself with my other fist.

I sparred with my uncle for a few minutes. Then I asked Miguel another question that had been bothering me since that morning.

"Tío, what would you do if you had to fight a group of guys?"

"Oh, that's much harder," he said. "One thing you always want to do is watch your back. Don't let anyone get behind you."

"Do you use your feet to kick?"

"Sure, or your feet to run."

"Run?" I was shocked—and disappointed.

"Sure—run." Miguel laughed. "That's not such a cowardly thing. It's sometimes the smartest thing a person can do."

Mami came out of the kitchen with dinner, and Miguel began talking to her about a car he had seen that he wanted to help her buy.

"I have to get my driver's license first," Mami said, almost dropping the tortillas she had just warmed on the stove.

I knew my mother wanted a car. I smiled. Getting a car would not just help Mami. It might solve one of my problems. I could get a ride from her instead of having to take the bus. The cholos couldn't get me then.

53

EIGHT

AT school I noticed some wanna-bes staring at me. Manuel spotted them first. They were freshmen, all with shaved heads, baggy jeans, and starched white T-shirts. They walked the same, talked the same, and all wanted the same thing—to be a Tres Palmas homeboy.

I knew the requirements. They had to prove themselves by doing something "brave" like stealing a carton of cigarettes, dashing from a convenience store with a six-pack, or, even harder but much more respected, jacking a car. Then the wanna-bes were jumped into the gang.

One jumping-in I had witnessed in eighth grade had been disgusting. A group of eight Tres Palmas had circled a wanna-be behind Bargain Barn and then hit and kicked him for two minutes. If he withstood the violence, he was in the gang.

It was all so stupid and awful. Friends beating on friends. Manuel and I didn't need to punch each other to be friends.

The wanna-bes usually weren't dangerous. But they could be annoying. The wanna-bes stared at me in the halls and in the cafeteria. Three of them were in a couple of my classes. I ignored them.

"Don't mad-dog them," Manuel advised. "Just don't stare at them."

"I know," I said. "Mad-dogging will get me nowhere except in a fight." I had seen enough fights around campus that had resulted from students staring one another down.

"How do they even know you?"

"I don't know. Maybe Spooky told them to bug me."

That afternoon in English when I got my notebook out, I saw that someone had written "Tres Palmas" on it.

I showed Manuel. "How do you think some wanna-be got ahold of my notebook?"

"Don't let your stuff get out of your sight. Especially when we're doing group work."

I nodded. I should have known better.

Yet, the next day in English, I took off my shoes while I was reading. Mami had brought me home this pair of brown canvas slip-ons, like the surfers wear. I wasn't a surfer, and I didn't want to be one, but the shoes were cool. When the bell rang, I looked under my desk to put my shoes back on, and one was missing.

"What are you looking for?" Mrs. Cavanough said as I searched the book compartment underneath each desk.

"My shoe."

"Class, no one leaves until Paulo has his shoe back. I'm tired of this immature hide-and-seek game some of you do with other people's property."

Mrs. Cavanough was mad. But she had been mad all week after she discovered someone had stolen her videocassette of *Romeo and Juliet* off her desk. A week earlier, some kid had jacked her coffee mug. That was low. Who wants an old, chipped coffee mug? Whoever was stealing was probably doing it just to make her angry.

No one had the shoe. Mrs. Cavanough checked each student's backpack, but still no shoe.

I had to go to my last two classes of the day in my socks, carrying one shoe.

"I know how they did it," Manuel said after thinking about it. "Someone close to the door passed it to someone outside. Remember how we had the door open? And we were moving around getting supplies for our poster. The person with your shoe passed it off like in a track race to a junior gangster who walked by in the hallway."

I couldn't think of any other explanation, so I agreed.

"They're making my life miserable, these wanna-bes."

"They make everyone's life here miserable," Manuel agreed. "The regular students hate them. The teachers hate them. I bet even their own parents hate them."

I had never thought about the gangsters' parents. Did they have parents? What were their parents like? Did Spooky actually have a mother? I couldn't imagine Spooky hugging his mother or Loco sitting with his father watching TV.

"Do you think their parents actually buy them those huge clothes?"

"Probably." Manuel flipped the hair out of his face. "Strange, huh?"

We watched a wanna-be with clown-size pants and a long white T-shirt struggle down the hallway. He would pull up his dragging pants, shuffle a bit, and then stop to adjust the waist. Pull, shuffle, adjust. Pull, shuffle, adjust.

"Why would anyone want to wear clothes that huge?" I asked.

"That's a simple one. They like the big clothes because it's easier to conceal their weapons."

"Where'd you hear that?" I said.

"From my dad who heard it from a cop. Makes sense, doesn't it?" Manuel said.

"Well, that guy could have an assault rifle in his clothing and we wouldn't know it," I agreed.

That week when I was leaving the lunch line carrying my root beer, burrito, chips, and apple on a tray, a group of wanna-bes surrounded me. I wasn't looking up because I had too much to balance. All of a sudden, the tray was flying out of my hands. My drink spilled all over my shirt, my burrito was stepped on, the chips were crushed, and the apple was gone.

When Gene, the campus security officer, made it through the crowd, I couldn't see the boys anymore. They had disappeared. "Who knocked into you?" Gene said in a bored voice.

I shrugged. Why go into it? He couldn't help me. There are so many wanna-bes that no way would I find the right ones, even if I had gotten a good look at them.

On Friday, when I got back from the field after P.E. class, I discovered my gym locker had been forced open. I pulled out my clothes; they were shredded. My shirt had holes everywhere. My blue jeans were cut and ripped into pieces. My socks had holes gouged in them. At the bottom of the locker, I found my Nikes. Someone had taken a knife and sliced through them. Even the shoelaces were cut.

Manuel came into the locker room after me. He kept flipping his hair back as he stared at the mess. "Wanna-bes?"

"Who else? Do you have any clothes I could borrow?"

"Just my jacket. Here."

I wore my P.E. clothes for the rest of the day.

I didn't know if I should show my mother the clothes. She would be scared sick. And she'd ask all kinds of questions about who would do this and why. Then I'd have to tell her about the wall. I threw the shredded clothes into the trash. I'd have to wear the shoes with the holes in them until I could find a way to get Mami to buy me another pair.

NINE

NIKKA needed to walk. I could tell she was restless. She wouldn't sit down by the couch. She went to the back door and whined; then she went to the front door and whined.

I checked the street. Everything looked quiet. I looked at the clock. It was early. The Tres Palmas homeboys were probably sleeping in on Saturday. I figured they partied until late on the weekends.

Mami was practicing driving with Miguel. She was going shopping afterward, and I knew she wouldn't be home until the afternoon.

I pulled down Nikka's leash. She scratched at the door when she saw it. "You're ready for a walk, aren't you, girl?" I said, fastening the leash on to her collar.

Nikka took off at a fast pace, pulling me slightly. She wasn't a huge dog, 70 pounds or so, but she was strong. And fast. I let her lead. She went straight to Colima Park.

When the park had been open, I used to let

her run there. She liked the hilly mounds and the trees. She used to bark at the ground squirrels, but after a rabid squirrel had been discovered, county officials had poisoned the squirrels by putting gas bombs into their tunnels. I didn't exactly miss them. They had started to overrun the park. Wherever I sat, one would pop up and scare me. I wondered if Nikka missed the squirrels. She would run from one tunnel opening to another, barking and waiting for the squirrels to come up.

I slipped through one of the holes cut in the chain-link fence that now surrounded the park. The grass was dead, and the plants were brown. After the county closed the park, no one watered it anymore. Most of the playground equipment was missing except for the metal slide that was covered with graffiti.

Nikka pulled at her leash, telling me she wanted to run. I unclipped the leash, and she was off—smelling, running, and exploring.

I examined the swing set. Papi had brought me here when I was a toddler and had swung me on this swing set. The swings now were cut away. Someone had taken the chains and thrown them up on the top bar. They wrapped around the bar like a thick cobra.

From the southern side of the park, I heard

voices. I turned to see white shirts and baggy pants. Cholos. They were entering the park through another hole in the fence. I checked for the opening I had come through. I would have to walk straight out in the middle to reach it. Should I take the chance?

No, it was better to stay low, to find a spot where the gangsters wouldn't see me. I moved to the building that housed the restrooms and crouched behind a rusty drinking fountain. From where I was, I couldn't see Nikka, and that worried me. She must be at the north end of the park, I thought.

The voices were coming closer. The gangsters were headed in my direction. I didn't stand up; I inched my way to the door of the women's restroom. The boards covering the door had been torn away. Perhaps I could get inside.

Still in a crouch, I pushed. The door swung open with only a slight sound.

I slipped into the restroom and headed for a stall. I chose the last one on the wall. I kept myself from gagging from the odor and filth. People had been using the bathroom since the park had been closed. Someone had been living in it. I could tell from the mound of clothing and the mildewy sleeping bag in one corner.

Trash was everywhere, and cigarette butts filled the sink. I pulled myself into one corner of the stall and closed my eyes to the mess. How long will I have to wait until I can get out of here? I thought. I'm never bringing Nikka here again. Never.

The gangsters were outside. I could hear three different voices.

"Is it good stuff?"

"Real good."

"How much?"

"Twenty."

"No, not here. Inside."

A drug deal—probably for crank, the drug of choice for many gangsters.

The door was opening. I heard feet shuffling and some swearing. They were complaining about the smell. Good. Maybe they wouldn't stay.

"Let's see it."

I could hear a shuffling of paper. There was a silence—a long silence.

Then rapid footsteps and BANG—the door to my stall was kicked open. Three faces peered at me. Each one looked identical because of the shaved heads, but gradually I could sort out the three. They were Tres Palmas homies—Spider, Ghost, and another one I couldn't identify. All were Loco's friends.

"Where you from?" Ghost said.

I knew the right answer. "Nowhere." *No gang. No neighborhood. Nowhere.* I spoke with as strong a Spanish accent as I could.

"He's a stupid wetback," No Name said.

"What are you doing here?"

I slowly stood up.

"I said, what you doing here?"

What was the right answer? I thought.

"Hanging out."

"In the toilet? What—you a pervert?" Spider made an obscene gesture, and the others laughed.

I took a step toward the door.

"You aren't going nowhere," Spider said.

I lunged for the gap between No Name and Ghost. I made it to the door before I was tackled. I landed on my side in a pile of trash, pulling No Name down with me. He struggled up, cussing and kicking at the trash he had touched. His crisp white T-shirt was smeared with a blackish filth.

I pulled myself up and leaned against the door of the first stall. I was just a few feet from the exit, but the door was closed and Spider was leaning against it.

"Just do him now," No Name said, pulling at his shirt and hitting at the dirt streak.

I watched as Spider's hand went for the pocket in his huge oversized pants. I remembered how Manuel had told me why the gangbangers liked to wear big clothes. *A gun? No, probably a knife.*

Spider's hand stopped. He raised his other hand up and motioned for No Name and Ghost to be quiet.

There was a noise at the door—nothing loud, but definitely a noise. Almost a breathing, or a scratching.

Spider motioned the others to get ready. He opened the door a crack and peered out. Then he swung the door open.

I saw legs of brown fur and then a mouth of white, jagged teeth. Spider was screaming.

I jumped for the door and ran. I turned around once. Ghost had taken off for an opening in the fence. Only No Name had stayed with Spider, who was trying to beat down Nikka. Her jaws were attached to one of Spider's thighs.

The hole in the fence was in front of me. I yelled for Nikka and burst through the opening. I didn't have to call again. Nikka was behind, pumping to catch up.

We didn't stop until we reached the front door. I fumbled with the key so much I had to take three deep breaths to control my shaking.

Finally we were inside. Nikka stood panting, her tongue lolling to the right.

"You were great," I said. Her brown eyes looked into mine as I rubbed her shoulders and head. Sweat ran from my hair and rolled down my nose and cheeks, but I felt elated. "You read my mind, didn't you? You knew I needed you."

I got Nikka some water and then treated her to a hunk of chicken Mami had cooked yesterday. I considered making myself a quesadilla, but my stomach was still lurching.

I wondered how badly injured Spider was. Would he need to get stitches? He wouldn't dare tell the police whose dog had bit him. Not when I could tell about the attempted murder or whatever it was going to be and the drug deal. No, he would say it was some stray dog. He'd probably get rabies shots.

I laughed for the first time in a week. Nikka seemed startled by the sound and moved close to me. I buried my face in her brown chest and laughed until her fur was wet from my tears.

TEN

MAMI had been studying for her driver's test.

"Paulo, did you know I can take the written test in Spanish?" she said, showing me the test booklet. "Edgar told me the State of California offers the driver's test in a person's native language. Amazing, yes?"

I peered over her shoulder at the booklet. I hoped Mami passed the test. And soon.

Mami showed me the Sunday *Times* she had bought that morning so she could look at the auto section.

"I found a Plymouth station wagon for only $700," Mami said, pointing at the ad. "And Heriberto said he would check the car before I bought it to make sure the engine is okay."

"Good. He'll make sure you won't get ripped off, Mami." I pulled the front section of the newspaper toward me. A small headline had caught my eye.

Dog Bite Victim Arrested on Warrant

It wasn't a good day for Jorge Calderone yesterday. First, he was bitten by a dog—severely enough that he required stitches. But after Calderone, 18, checked into Eastland Hospital's emergency room for treatment, police, who were called to make a report on the dog bite, arrested Calderone on an outstanding warrant.

Calderone, a Puente resident, was wanted on an outstanding warrant for driving while intoxicated. He had failed to show for a September 20 court appearance.

When Detective Ted Jevis ran a computer check on Calderone, he discovered the warrant and arrested Calderone after doctors closed a dog bite on his thigh with 23 stitches.

"It was a bad bite. It definitely needed care," Dr. José Gutierrez, the physician who treated Calderone, said.

Calderone told police that he attempted to break up a dogfight and was injured when one dog turned on him.

I reread the article. Spider, a.k.a. Jorge Calderone, was in jail. And he had lied to the police about the bite.

For a second, I thought about going to the police with the real story. Maybe Spider would be charged with attempted murder. But I couldn't go to the police. If I did, I'd never survive. I had heard what gangsters do to people who talk to police.

Spider was gone, but Ghost and No Name were still around, plus Loco and Spooky. Add the wanna-bes to that, and I was greatly outnumbered. I needed a weapon. I'd have to protect myself.

When my mother was in the shower, I searched the kitchen drawers for the sharpest and smallest knife I could find. It would have to fit into the small side pocket of my backpack when I went to school. That way no one would see it when I opened the main part of the bag to pull out my books.

I knew I could get into trouble at school for carrying a knife. But I wouldn't get caught. And I needed that knife, especially after what had happened. I wished I could talk to Tío Miguel about how to handle myself in a knife fight. But if I asked him that, he'd get suspicious.

I picked up one of Mami's smaller meat knives and put it into my backpack. I hoped I'd never have to use it. But just maybe pulling it out when I was being hassled would scare the gangsters away.

I showed Manuel the knife when we were in the restroom at school. "I hope you don't get caught with that," he said, looking to make sure no one else was around.

"I know. But what else can I do? I don't want to get killed. And you know that's what Tres Palmas will do to me."

"Couldn't you have just ignored the graffiti? It's only a wall," Manuel said after we returned to our classroom.

I felt the fire return to my stomach, the same fire I'd felt when Spooky and Loco had spray-painted the wall the first time. "No, it's my wall. They can't just claim whatever they want. My mother and I worked for that wall."

Manuel looked puzzled, but I couldn't explain how Mami worked so hard at her job and didn't take time off even when she was sick so that we could afford to have that house, that yard . . . that wall. I couldn't explain about the pictures of me with my father in front of that wall. The wall was in the background of the photograph where Papi was teaching me to ride a bike. In another, Mami and Papi were dressed for Mass, and I was in my stroller. My favorite photograph was one Mami took of Papi dressed in shorts and no shirt planting the flowered tree by the wall.

"It's like . . . when they spray-paint the wall, it's as if they're inside our house, spraying our living room. Does that make sense?"

Manuel shook his head. I sank lower in my seat.

I wondered if Tío Miguel would understand. I wished I could talk to him about it, but Tío Miguel would tell Mami. And Mami would be furious that I was fighting with cholos. Since I was little, she had told me to avoid them.

But so far Mami didn't know what was going on with me and Tres Palmas. She'd seen my Nikes with the holes, and she thought the shoes were wearing out because I was playing soccer in them. I was glad she didn't check my shoes any closer. We went shopping, and she bought me a new pair. My new ones were nice—black and gray and a size larger. That meant I was growing taller, which made me happy. I wanted to be as tall as my father.

Other than that shopping trip, Mami and I were doing things separately. It was strange. Lately Mami had been leaving me alone. She spent time on the phone talking to Edgar.

And, most amazing, Mami had colored her

hair. She said she didn't like the gray streaks anymore.

I knew what was happening, but I didn't like to think about it. I mean, Edgar seemed okay, but I didn't like how my mother acted around him. She was so different, so talkative and smiley.

He came over to the house one evening. He drove a pretty decent Lincoln. When he came to the door, I was surprised to realize how short he was. He was only a few inches taller than my mother. His hair was black, really black, and his skin was dark. He looked more Indian than Mexican.

"Hello, Paulo," he said, shaking my hand in a firm grasp.

I said only enough to be polite and then retreated to my room. I could hear them talking and laughing in the kitchen. Mami was making dinner for him. For me, too, but I knew the dinner was really for him because she was cooking *carne asada*. We have steak only on special occasions, so I knew this meal had to be for him.

That was okay. I wasn't jealous.

But later, sitting at the dining room table with Mami laughing and Edgar cutting the steak and complimenting Mami on her cooking, I couldn't help taking a look at Papi's photograph sitting on the trunk in the corner.

What would he say about all this? Seven years he had been gone. Had Mami forgotten about him? I hadn't, and I had only been in second grade when he died. If I could remember him that well, she'd better not forget about him.

As soon as I could without being rude, I escaped back to my bedroom. My mother and Edgar didn't seem to notice.

For a week there was no more graffiti on the wall. I didn't see Spooky, Loco, or anyone. The wanna-bes still stared, but I always looked away. Sometimes I noticed Albert looking at me in class, but he always looked at the floor when I looked back at him.

Albert rarely talked to anyone in class. Once at the beginning of the school year, Manuel and I were placed in a group with Albert for a presidential election project. He didn't say much, but he recorded the group's work. He had neat handwriting. He seemed to be a good student too. He had given us his phone number in case we remembered anything else he needed to write for our group's project.

For part of the project, the students had to ask their parents which candidate they had voted for in the last election. Only Ben Rodriguez's father, who was born in East L.A., had voted. My mom can't vote, of course, because she's not an American citizen.

"Did your parents vote?" Manuel asked Albert.

Head down, Albert mumbled, "Nah, my mom don't do stuff like that."

Mr. Hilbert, our teacher, hadn't graded us on whether or not our parents had voted. A good thing, too, because most of us would have gotten Fs. He gave our group an A– on our project. He wrote on the grading sheet, "Neatly done."

Manuel had pointed to Mr. Hilbert's comment and said to Albert, "Hey, thanks."

It was the first time I'd ever seen Albert smile.

The school newspaper was delivered every Friday in social studies classes. Mr. Hilbert always passed it out and made us read every article. Usually we had to write about some topic we found in the paper.

That afternoon Mr. Hilbert had us write

about metal detectors. Some of the schools in Los Angeles were getting metal detectors to discourage students from bringing weapons to class. Our topic was this: Should La Vista High School use metal detectors?

"What do they think students bring to school? Uzi submachine guns?" Ben Rodriguez said.

"Yeah, sometimes they do," said Ramon Telles, "but they're really looking for handguns and knives. I heard that from my cousin who's a security guard at a school."

With a start, I remembered my knife. It was still in my backpack. I had just left it there.

I had trouble getting started on Mr. Hilbert's assignment. At first I wanted to write that metal detectors were wrong, that they took away students' privacy and made school like a prison.

But I kept thinking about Spooky and the other gangbangers, including the wanna-bes. I'd feel safer if they were checked out each day with a metal detector. I wouldn't have to worry about watching my back in school. Having to watch my back in my neighborhood was bad enough. But at least I could relax at school.

I wrote the assignment Mr. Hilbert had asked for. I agreed with using metal detectors in schools. As I wrote my composition, I glanced over at Albert. He wasn't writing. He was staring at the floor.

I wondered what he thought about his brother. Did he want to become just like Spooky when he was older? Did he know about Spooky's graffiti? Why hadn't he bothered me? He didn't act like the other wanna-bes. Maybe he stayed out of his brother's business.

The bell rang, and I turned in my rough draft for credit. I knew I'd get it returned tomorrow with some comments from Mr. Hilbert, and then I'd rewrite it as homework. That was what Mr. Hilbert called the "writing process." You never really finished an assignment. It was always written, rewritten, read, commented on, rewritten, read, commented on, rewritten.

By the afternoon in Mrs. Cavanough's English class, I was getting tired. It was hot in the classroom, and the teachers had been working us like mules. I guess teachers do that when it gets close to state exam time.

Mrs. Cavanough had us reading *Lord of the Flies*, a really interesting book about a bunch of kids stranded on an island. They started off okay by setting up rules and leaders, but then they got wild and primitive and started fighting one another. Their behavior at the end when they acted like savages was disgusting. They chanted these sick songs like "Kill the beast. Drink his blood," and they jammed a pig's head on a stick.

During one period we argued whether or not the story was realistic. A bunch of the kids said no way, that kids wouldn't act like that. "They wouldn't get all savage and murderous," this blonde girl said. "That's not natural."

Usually Albert was so quiet in class, we forgot he was there. He didn't sit close to us like in Mr. Hilbert's class. In English he was at the back of the room. But today he spoke up.

"They would. Believe me. They'd go savage real fast." He said it almost angrily. Mrs. Cavanough looked surprised, but she kept the discussion going by calling on Ramon Telles.

I kept looking at Albert until our eyes met. Then we both quickly looked away.

"Take out your yellow marker and highlight these passages," Mrs. Cavanough said that afternoon. "For the final exam, you'll need to explain the significance of these passages in *Lord of the Flies.*"

I reached into the side pocket of my backpack where I keep my markers. I felt a sharp pain and brought my hand up to my face. Blood rolled down my palm.

"Sick! How'd you do that?" Ben Rodriguez said.

I sat like an idiot staring at my hand. I had gashed two fingers pretty deep.

"Mrs. Cavanough," Martha Cervantes called. "Paulo's bleeding. He's getting blood everywhere."

Mrs. Cavanough turned faster than I had ever seen her move. "How did that happen, Paulo?"

Martha was peering into my backpack. She pulled back the front of the side pocket.

"He cut himself with this, Mrs. Cavanough," Martha said, slowly pulling out my knife by the handle.

Mrs. Cavanough was handing me gauze from the first-aid kit she keeps in her top desk drawer. As I wrapped up my fingers, she called the office.

Within minutes, Gene, the campus security officer, was at the door. Mrs. Cavanough pointed to me. "There he is."

I stood up, feeling stupid and embarrassed. Manuel helped me put my notebook and books into my backpack. He handed my backpack to Gene.

"Don't forget this," Martha said, handing Gene the knife. Gene held the handle of the knife between his finger and thumb and followed me to the office.

La Vista doesn't have a full-time nurse, but I was lucky that it was the nurse's day on campus. She goes to five different high schools, one each day of the week.

"You can get by with just a butterfly bandage, or if your parents want, they can take you to the emergency room for a couple of stitches on each finger," the nurse said after examining me.

I knew my mother couldn't afford an emergency room visit. "The bandage will be fine," I said.

"You'll have a scar on each," she said.

I nodded. I didn't care about scars. Not on my fingers.

When the nurse finished cleaning the cuts and applying the bandages, I was ready to go back to class. I asked her for a pass to fifth period.

"You can't go back to class," she said, surprised.

"Why? I'm fine."

"The knife."

"Oh." I wondered what my punishment would be. Perhaps I would have Work School. That wouldn't be too bad. I'd just have to come to school early Saturday morning and pick up trash and sweep hallways. Big deal. I could handle that. Maybe Tío Miguel would drive me to school, or I could take the public bus since the school bus, of course, didn't run on weekends.

Mrs. Porter, the assistant principal, was standing in the doorway of the nurse's office.

"Ready?" she said.

"He's fine," the nurse said.

"Come with me, Paulo," Mrs. Porter said.

I went with her to her office. I had never been in trouble at La Vista before. Except for when my counselor scheduled my classes, I had never seen the offices inside the guidance building before.

Mrs. Porter motioned for me to sit down in a chair across from her desk.

"Paulo, you know we have a policy about bringing weapons on campus. Every year you and all the students sign a contract stating that you understand our rules and that you will suffer the consequences if you break them."

I nodded. In September, a counselor had come to Mr. Hilbert's class and explained the rules and made us sign this contract.

Mrs. Porter pulled out a copy of the contract. "Read rule number three and the consequence."

I scanned the sheet. "Students shall not

bring any weapon, or object that appears to simulate a weapon, on campus. Weapons include but are not limited to firearms, knives, nunchuks, chains, bats, or clubs."

Then I read the consequences: "Students who violate this rule shall be expelled."

My eyes blurred. I stared at Mrs. Porter, but I couldn't focus on her face.

Mrs. Porter's voice seemed to come from the ceiling. "I need to talk to your mother about your expulsion, Paulo. How can we contact her?"

ELEVEN

WHEN Mami came into the office, I knew by the confused look on her face that she had no idea what was going on.

"Are you hurt, m'ijo?"

I shook my head.

"Did somebody try to hurt you with a knife?"

Mrs. Porter stepped into the office. "Do you need a Spanish translator, Mrs. Gomez?" she asked.

Mami shook her head. "What happened to my son?"

I realized that this was the first time my mother had ever been to my school. She doesn't go to Back-to-School Night or things like that. And I had always been a good student. I had never been assigned detention or received an unsatisfactory citizenship grade. How could I explain?

Mrs. Porter showed my mother my bandaged hand. "It's not a bad cut, Mrs. Gomez, but I need you to look at this." She pointed to the knife on her desk and told Mami I had carried it in my backpack.

"My kitchen knife? Why did you bring that to school?" Mami asked, her face looking gray.

I hung my head. I tried to think of something to say. "I brought it to cut my food, you know, apples and stuff," I said in Spanish. "I'm sorry, Mami."

"We have a school discipline policy that we follow, Mrs. Gomez. We absolutely prohibit any weapons, and that includes knives. Your son has been a good student here, but we must start an expulsion proceeding. In the meantime, he must stay home. He's not allowed back on this campus," Mrs. Porter said.

"What is this expulsion?" Mami said.

"*Expulsion* means that he will not be able to attend this school for the rest of this school year. We will assign him to another school in the district. At the end of one complete school year, he will be allowed to return to La Vista if he has a good record at the other school."

I blinked my eyes to clear them. A new school. No friends. Strange teachers. Strange classrooms.

"What school?" I asked. My voice sounded like a sick cricket's, all raspy and shrill.

"New Frontiers."

I knew about that school. It was the school for the losers, the kids who couldn't handle regular schoolwork or had truancy problems.

"Paulo must go home with you. In three days I'll call you and give you the papers to enroll him in New Frontiers," Mrs. Porter said.

Mami and I walked out silently. I carried my backpack, but Mrs. Porter had confiscated the knife to use as evidence in my expulsion hearing.

We walked to the bus stop. I noticed that Mami's hands shook as she paid for our fares. She didn't talk to me until we were home and inside with the door shut and double-latched.

"Now, Paulo, you tell me why you would do such a stupid thing. You didn't need that knife to cut food with."

I couldn't keep up such a stupid lie so I told her I was trying to be a tough guy, to impress some cholos who were messing with me.

"To bring a knife to school like a . . . like a . . . bad boy, a criminal, a stupid banty rooster."

Mami's voice trembled, but her eyes were black, and she held her hands in fists. I moved away from her. She had never hit me before, but today I wasn't sure she wouldn't.

I told her about Spooky and the others who were writing on the wall. I told her how the wanna-bes bothered me at school and how I had painted over the graffiti, but I didn't tell her about the incident in the bathroom at Colima Park. No way. She'd book us a flight to Mexico tomorrow, she'd be so scared.

"It's just a wall, Paulo. Why would you take on a group of cholos? You don't mess with boys like that."

"I know, Mami. I made a mistake."

"You are usually such a smart boy. And this was stupid. Dangerous. You don't cause troubles in your neighborhood. You know that."

I reached out for Nikka and petted her. Just touching her made me feel better. Mami watched me touching Nikka.

"You don't cause any problems at the new school. If you do, I'll give Nikka to Lilian's boy."

"Mami? You'd do that?" I had never heard my mother threaten me.

Mami's dark eyes stared into mine. "Yes, I would. I would do whatever I needed to keep you from being a bad boy."

I pulled Nikka into my room and shut the door. "Don't worry, Nikka. I won't lose you," I whispered, stroking Nikka's brown fur. "It's not even a possibility." I repeated the words again and again until she and I were both asleep.

TWELVE

MAMI must have told Edgar about my expulsion because when he came over the next day, he wanted to talk to me in my room.

He tried to be calm and low-key, but that made him seem even more annoying. He told me how he had gotten into trouble in school, how he had learned to leave people alone, and how carrying weapons is a sign of weakness.

"It's better to solve a problem using this," he said, tapping his head.

"Yadda, yadda, yadda, yeah," I felt like saying, but of course I didn't. If I was rude, I'd get into more trouble with Mami.

Edgar could see he couldn't get much out of me. I just said, "Yeah, sure, you're right. I know. I agree." Finally he left me alone and found my mother who had been conveniently busy in the kitchen.

I was trying to be especially nice to Mami. I didn't like how she had looked at Nikka. I had never known Mami to be so serious about anything.

I could see Edgar and Mami talking in the kitchen. From the few words I heard, I knew they were talking about me. Then Edgar leaned over and patted Mami on her shoulder. He kept his hand there as they talked.

It was suffocating in my house.

I took Nikka for a walk. We visited every neighbor on the street. We watched Heriberto work on a Chevy engine. We visited Concha. Osa was inside with her puppies. We admired Antonio Garcia's tomatoes growing on wire frames on the side of his house. I bought a bag of *chicharrones* for two bucks and shared them with Nikka.

When anyone asked me how I was doing, I said, "Great. Wonderful. How are you?" I *was* doing wonderful. Who wouldn't be with a dog like mine, a neighborhood filled with friends, and a chance to start a new school and make new friends? I was feeling *wonderful*.

When I got home, I took Nikka into the backyard. I kicked the metal trash can a couple of times, and I felt even more wonderful. I hurled my basketball at the garage door as hard as I could just to hear the heavy clang it made. I felt wonderful. I kicked dirt at the chickens, which made them take off running, and I felt even more wonderful. Nikka moved away from me and sat on the back steps watching me.

Mami called me in for dinner.

"Wonderful," I said. "Wonderful."

I had to take a city bus to get to New Frontiers High School. I went to the office and got my schedule. The school was smaller than La Vista, and the students looked different. Here, almost every student wore baggy pants, Pendleton shirts, and basketball shoes. The guys all had shaved heads. It looked as if I was the only one with hair. I felt out of place in my jeans and blue T-shirt.

Students openly smoked in the parking lot. At La Vista, smokers had to sneak around. I guess New Frontiers had bigger problems than smokers.

I found my first class, which was math. I presented my enrollment slip to the teacher, a thin, bald man named Mr. Kitridge. I found a chair close to the front and sat down.

Mr. Kitridge handed me a textbook. It was one I had worked out of in eighth grade. I wondered if all the classes would be easier at New Frontiers. Great. Not only did I get put into a school for troublemakers, I got put in remedial classes.

I heard a voice behind me say, "Well, it's Paulo, the Wall-boy."

I looked back to see Spooky.

Spooky went to New Frontiers.

It had never occurred to me that the gangsters of Tres Palmas would go to that school, but it made sense. New Frontiers was for losers, and Spooky would have been kicked out of La Vista High School long ago.

Spooky's friend, Loco, was in the class too.

"Look at the new kid," Spooky said, pointing to me.

I sunk low in the chair. How would I survive the day?

I couldn't concentrate on anything in the lesson Mr. Kitridge was presenting, even though we had covered integers last year. All I could think about was how I could get out without a fight.

When the bell rang, I lagged behind so I could be the last one out of the classroom.

As Spooky walked to the door, he popped me on the back of the head with the palm of his hand. "You're gone, Wall-boy. You don't mess with Tres Palmas and live."

I waited until Spooky and Loco had disappeared down the hall. Then I headed for the entrance of the school. Once outside the gate, I ran.

I remembered what Tío Miguel had said. Sometimes running is the smartest thing to do. And at that moment, I knew I needed to run.

For the next few weeks, I lived a lie. I got up, got dressed for school, and ate breakfast with my books beside me. Mami would hug me good-bye and say, "Have a good day at school, m'ijo."

I would nod and take a bigger bite out of my egg burrito. When Mami was gone, I would turn on the TV and watch the morning news programs. At noon I would make myself lunch and watch the talk shows. I took Nikka for a walk and got the groceries. I visited the chickens in the backyard. I weeded the lawn in the back and took out the trash. I washed all the dishes and watched more television.

When Mami came home, she would talk to me as she made dinner. "How are your classes? Have you made any new friends?"

I would tell her about my day. How I ate lunch with this new guy, Antonio. How I wrote an essay on capital punishment for my social science class. How I was meeting people who rode the city bus every day at the same time, and how I liked my teachers at the new school. All lies.

I couldn't believe Mami wasn't suspicious. As I told her the lies, my voice sounded so strange and awful. Couldn't she hear the lies in my voice? Maybe she didn't notice because her friend—no, her boyfriend—Edgar was calling her all the time and she was thinking about that.

My lies were spreading. Heriberto had seen me around during school hours and had asked me what I was doing at home on a school day. I had lied and told him it was a teacher conference day. From then on I knew I had to avoid him in the mornings. He'd suspect something if he saw me at home during the day again. And Heriberto definitely would say something to Mami if he suspected I was ditching school.

At night, I would cover my head with my pillow and wonder how my life could possibly have gotten this bad. What a fool I had been to take a knife to school. I'm a liar, a coward, a loser, I thought. Even reaching down to pet Nikka didn't make me feel any better.

Manuel called me that first week to ask me about the new school. I told him the truth.

"You mean Spooky and Loco go there? No

wonder you stopped going. You'd be killed," Manuel said.

"I know. But now I'm a prisoner in my own house."

"Why don't you spend the weekend at my house?" Manuel said.

"Sure," I said, eager for a chance to get out.

Mami wasn't happy about letting me go to Manuel's. She felt I still should be punished for what had happened with the knife.

"But, Mami," I argued, "I'm being punished enough, having to go to another school. I've learned my lesson. And besides, Edgar is taking you to that mariachi party on Saturday. Then Sunday you're going to a baby shower with Lilian. If you let me stay with Manuel, you won't have to worry about me being home alone all weekend."

Finally Mami agreed to let me go. I gave Nikka a good-bye rub of her head and then took the bus to Manuel's house.

I swam in the pool at Manuel's apartment complex and played ping-pong at the Boys Club nearby. For the first time in weeks, I was able to laugh. Manuel did imitations of country western singers, and I practiced my imitation of Ricky Martin. Manuel and I didn't talk about Spooky and Loco and Tres Palmas. He could tell that I didn't want to think about them.

I did chores with Manuel and helped wash his dad's car. Manuel and I walked to the AM/PM market to buy soft drinks.

"This is the first time in a long time that I'm able to walk without having to look around at everybody," I said.

"You mean watching your back, stuff like that?"

I nodded. "Lately, it seems like my world has shrunk. You know what I mean? I can't go many places outside of my house."

"School's been boring without you," Manuel said, opening the door to the market and letting me go in first. "I eat lunch with Ben Rodriguez, but it's not the same."

I didn't answer, but I understood what Manuel was saying about our friendship.

It was a perfect weekend except that I missed Nikka. The toughest time was at night. I slept on the floor with a pile of blankets next to Manuel's bed. At first Manuel and I talked, but after he fell asleep, I thought about Nikka. I wondered if my mother was letting her sleep inside my room. She probably put Nikka out. She still liked the Mexican way where animals stayed outside.

I wondered what it would be like to be part

of Manuel's family. It'd be nice to have brothers and sisters. Manuel always had someone to talk to, and when he came home after school, there was always someone in his house. I had Nikka, though, so I wasn't alone.

Manuel's family had a cat that never left their apartment. Cats are okay, but they're not as fun as dogs. Manuel's cat slept half the day. And she ignored people. It was as if humans didn't really exist in her world. Dogs are always aware of people. They seem to want a human friendship. Cats couldn't care less.

I fell asleep thinking about Nikka and how I could tell when she was happy or bored or worried just by looking at the shine in her eyes.

Manuel's father gave me a ride home Sunday afternoon. I thanked Manuel's parents for the weekend and then sat in the backseat of the car thinking about how some families are so different.

Manuel's parents were from El Salvador. They were strict with their children. They couldn't get food from the refrigerator without asking their parents' permission. Manuel had to ask his mother if he could use the telephone.

At a stoplight, Manuel and I watched a boy in baggy pants walk by. "What would your parents do if you bought a pair of baggies?" I asked in a low voice.

Manuel laughed. "I wouldn't. I hate them."

"No, just say that you did like them. And you started wearing big pants and Pendletons and shaving your head. That kind of stuff. What would happen?"

"I know the answer to that. My father's already told us that if we start acting like cholos, he'll send us to El Salvador to live with our *abuelo*, and that won't be fun. Grandpa will put us to work picking coffee beans."

"Really? Your parents would send you away?"

"No question about it. One of my cousins was sent to El Salvador after he stole beer from a mini-market. He was with some gangsters."

I wondered if Mami was considering sending me to Mexico. Maybe after the knife thing, she had thought about it.

Was I a bad person? Maybe I was like a gangster, fighting over territory. After all, it was just a wall. It really wasn't mine. Mami and I only rented the house. We weren't the owners of the wall.

Did I paint over the graffiti because the cholos were invading my territory? The thought was scary to me. I didn't want to be even remotely like the gangsters, but maybe I was.

Why didn't I follow Manuel's advice and just leave the wall alone? By painting over the graffiti, I had taken on the gang. A smart person would have left the whole thing alone. Pick your battles, Tío Miguel had told me.

Maybe I had picked the wrong battle.

THIRTEEN

I kept myself busy that next week by drawing a picture of Nikka. Mr. Shagallini had taught us how to use charcoal, and I sketched a rough of Nikka as she sat next to me in the living room. Then I used charcoal to cover the pencil and add contrast. The drawing came out pretty good. I caught Nikka's expression with her mouth slightly open and her eyes looking right at me. I was surprised. Maybe Mr. Shagallini was right and I did have some talent.

I showed it to Nikka. She just sniffed the paper and turned away. "You have no appreciation for art, my friend," I said. I placed the drawing in the dining room next to Papi's photograph. Mami noticed it right away when she got home.

She looked at it for a long time and then said, "You should think about becoming an artist, m'ijo."

I felt pretty good about the drawing. After everything that had happened, I was really glad

I drew it. Mami bought me a frame for it later, and now it's hanging up in my bedroom.

Mami got her car the following week. Tío Miguel was showing her how to drive. I had never seen my mother so happy and proud.

It wasn't a wonderful car, just a 13-year-old station wagon with a couple of minor dents and in need of a paint job. Still, the interior was good, Tío Miguel said, and the engine was fine. Heriberto had given the car his one-word approval—"Okay."

I sat in the passenger seat and looked around. My mother looked at the engine as Tío Miguel explained how to check the oil.

Mami had a lot to learn, I realized, but I could tell she was excited. She needed a car. Sometimes she got off work after 6:00. The warehouse was in downtown L.A., and sometimes she waited at the bus stop in the dark. I worried about her getting mugged—or worse.

Nikka stood by the open door and sniffed the inside of the car. "Mami, can I let Nikka in?"

Mami hesitated. "Okay, but you'll have to vacuum my seat covers if she sheds much."

I slid over and Nikka jumped in. Nikka had missed me last weekend, Mami said, and had sat by the wall watching for me.

I gripped the steering wheel and imagined driving. Where would I go? To Huntington Beach, perhaps, with a Frisbee for Nikka to play with and a cooler of drinks. I'd invite Manuel and maybe Ben Rodriguez. I'd find a clear, clean area of sand where I'd stretch out on my towel and absorb the sun. Nikka could run at the water's edge and snap at the tide.

Mami was at the car window. "Miguel is going to put on new tires. He wants to teach you how to change a tire."

I climbed out of the car.

Opening a portable toolbox, Tío Miguel pointed to a line of tools. "Find the lug wrench," he directed.

Mami smiled. "And, if there's time, Miguel, could you and Paulo clear out a spot for me in the garage? I need a place to put my car."

That evening my muscles ached as I stretched out in bed. From the swimming at Manuel's to the working with Tío Miguel, I had been busy. Miguel and I had put on two new tires, replacing the bad ones in the rear. Then we had started on the garage, but by dusk we had not yet cleared out a space big enough for Mami's car.

Miguel had too many tools and car parts to organize. Mami said she'd wait until next weekend for her space in the garage. She had parked her car in the driveway and carefully locked it. Miguel had given her a lock, which she hooked into the steering wheel to prevent theft.

Heriberto always said things had to be nailed down in our neighborhood or they'd get stolen. Once, about 4:00 a.m., Heriberto had caught some loser rummaging through the glove box in a van Heriberto had forgotten to lock. Heriberto grabbed a shovel and scared the guy, who dropped everything and took off running.

On the other hand, living in a neighborhood like mine wasn't bad if you wanted to get rid of stuff and didn't want to haul it away. Every Tuesday night about 11:00, the trash pickers came through our streets. They usually pushed stolen shopping carts and rummaged through the trash cans by the curbs.

Once Mami and I put out a ripped, moldy mattress. It was gone in an hour. I saw it later in someone's backyard. Some old guy with white whiskers was sleeping on it. The trash pickers took just about anything that had any value— broken chairs, headless dolls, holey tennis shoes, rusty bike parts, and glass jars. Tío Miguel called our neighborhood "Scavenger City." But Mami's car would be safe with the lock on the steering wheel.

I dropped my arm over the bed so I could pet Nikka. She was already sleeping, and I knew I would fall asleep easily tonight. Somehow, life seemed better today. Perhaps it was Mami's car, or perhaps it had been the easy weekend spent with Manuel, or perhaps it was the wag of Nikka's tail when she saw me after Manuel's father had dropped me off by the wall. Somehow, I had hope. Strange, how life tricks you like that.

The next morning, after my mother had said good-bye, I began cleaning the breakfast dishes. I thought about how I should spend the day. Mami assumed I would be at school, but maybe I could work on the garage some more and have a spot ready for her car when she came home. Of course, Mami might get suspicious that I could complete such a big job in the few hours after school.

As I rinsed my plate, I heard Mami calling my name. I peered out from the kitchen, and Mami motioned me outside.

I wondered what she had forgotten and what she needed me to do. Perhaps her car wouldn't start. That would be such a disappointment—having to take the bus to work on her first day with a car.

Mami was standing next to the car. She had

a strange look on her face, almost as if she couldn't talk. I walked outside and saw the writing—the Tres Palmas insignia—but not on the wall.

The words *Tres Palmas* were spray-painted in huge letters across the sides of the car, on the hood, and on the back.

I wanted to throw up.

"Get the hose, would you, Paulo? Let's try to spray it off."

I knew water wouldn't do it, but I didn't argue. I got the hose and sprayed the car while Mami scrubbed at the hideous letters with a rag. It was obvious that nothing would remove the paint.

For once, my mother seemed unsure of what to do. She stared at the car, her lips in an O, and blinked.

"I guess I'll have to drive it like that until Tío Miguel can paint it," she said.

"No, Mami, you can't. You're a target for a bullet. You can't drive anywhere but around our neighborhood in the car, certainly not to work."

"Why not? What do you mean—a bullet?"

I rubbed my eyes, and my voice got lower. "You go through some different neighborhoods on your way to work. Well, you go advertising where you are from, showing your colors, then

somebody from . . . say . . . Brown Brothers or
Magnolia Muthers or Walnut Projects is going to
shoot at the car."

"Gangsters will think I'm a rival?"

"Sure, with *Tres Palmas* sprayed all over
your car."

Mami shook her head. "This is a crazy world.
Sometimes I want so much to go back to
Mexico."

I walked back into the house with her. She
called work to tell her boss that she was going to
be late.

I got some primer paint from the garage and
lightly covered the writing. "Tío Miguel can fix
this, Mami. Don't worry," I said, brushing the
gray paint onto the car. "The primer will cover
the writing so at least you'll be okay driving
today."

My mother looked at her watch. "You're
going to be late for school, m'ijo."

My eyes never left the brush. I continued
painting and, as casually as I could, said, "Yes,
but I'll explain what happened to my teacher. I'll
take the 9:00 bus to school."

"I'll drive you," Mami said.

"No, Mami, don't bother. The bus is fine."

"No, if we hurry, I can get you to school by
8:30 so you won't miss much."

"But, Mami, I have to clean up after I finish painting. And I don't want to make you any later to work."

"I talked to Lilian, and she said she'd cover for me. No, I'm going to drive you to school."

My stomach lurched, but I finished painting over the *Tres Palmas*. I cleaned the brush, packed up my "school" books, and climbed into the car.

My mother drove slowly, but she did pretty well, I had to admit. At the entrance of the school, Mami pulled over. I checked the school grounds. Most of the students were in class, and I didn't see Spooky or Loco.

"Bye, Mami," I said. "Thanks for the ride."

I watched her drive off. She stopped at the stop sign and waved to me. I waited until her car was out of my sight, and then I turned to leave. I needed to get out of there before Spooky or Loco or any of the other Tres Palmas gangsters got a clue I was on campus.

But it was too late.

Spooky was strolling out of a classroom with what looked like an office pass in his hand. When he saw me, his face broke into a pleased grin.

He came toward me fast. I turned to run but whirled around and faced Spooky when I realized he was too close for me to safely escape. I remembered what Tío Miguel had said. *Watch your back.*

Spooky stopped a few feet from me. "*Qué pasa*, Wall-boy? Where you been?"

I didn't answer. My body was tense, ready for movement.

"You show me no respect, Wall-boy. That ain't cool."

Still I was silent.

"Wall-boy, answer me. Where you been?"

I didn't speak, and he didn't move.

Spooky stepped forward, his arms raised and eyes narrowed. "Come on, Wall-boy. You can't dis me and get away with it."

Just as Spooky's fist came forward, my fist shot out, hitting Spooky in the mouth. I blocked Spooky's fist with my other hand, just as Tío Miguel had shown me.

My second punch got Spooky in the stomach, and, as he bent over, I punched him hard on the back of his neck. Then I turned and ran.

I didn't look back until I was a mile away from the school. I caught the bus from the stop on the boulevard and rode all the way home.

Nikka was waiting by the wall. She greeted me with an anxious whine.

I hurried to our door and let myself in, and Nikka followed. I ran to the bathroom and looked at myself in the mirror. I still looked the same. Spooky hadn't gotten one punch in, but somehow I felt damaged, crushed.

I had never before fought like that. When I was young, I had wrestled around with friends, but I had never really fought anyone. When I was young and the boys at school fought during the soccer games, I would walk away. I never joined in.

My hands shook a bit as I petted Nikka. I stared at my hands. The one ached slightly from punching Spooky. The two scars on my fingers shone white against my brown skin. Those were my scars of stupidity.

This entire problem was my fault. If I hadn't brought the knife to school, if I hadn't yelled at the gangbangers to quit tagging my wall, if I had just left the graffiti on the wall . . .

Petting Nikka calmed me, and I felt myself relaxing as I talked to her and rubbed her head. I had to think clearly. I knew Spooky would get me back. I had gotten the better of him today, and there was no way Spooky could let that go. I had to work out some solution. But what?

That afternoon when I knew Manuel would

be home from school, I called him and told him the latest.

"You mean you actually duked it out—you punched him?"

"Twice. No, three times."

"He didn't hit you at all?"

"No."

"Oh, that's bad. If you had just let him pound you a little, maybe he'd stop harassing you."

"You mean, let him win one battle to end the war?"

"Yes," Manuel said. "Exactly."

"It wouldn't have worked. Guys like Spooky work on respect. If they respect you, they leave you alone."

"So you were teaching him a little respect by punching him?"

"It just happened. I didn't want to get punched, so I punched him."

"That's bad. Real bad. You know," Manuel said, a sympathetic tone in his voice, "some of these cholos are buying guns at the swap meets."

I felt my stomach twist again. "How'd you hear that?"

"My dad, from his cop friend. He told him that the cops are checking out the swap meets lately because they heard people are selling guns illegally from the backs of their vans or the trunks of their cars."

"Do you think they'll try a drive-by?"

My neighborhood had had one drive-by shooting already, a few years before. All the neighbors remembered it. A member of Cactus Posse had rented a home in Tres Palmas territory. When he started having parties at his house and inviting his posse over, Tres Palmas went after him. There was a mess of graffiti everywhere. Then Tres Palmas had driven by his house and fired a few bullets into his walls. No one was hurt, but the Cactus Posse guy moved away the next day, and the neighborhood returned to its normal state.

Manuel said, "You'd better sleep on the floor. You're safer there."

I was glad my mother's bedroom was at the back of the house. She would be safe sleeping that far from the street.

That evening I rolled my blankets and pulled my pillow onto the ground next to Nikka. She gave me a surprised look and nudged me with her nose. I smiled and lay down beside her. "Don't hog the blankets, Nikka."

FOURTEEN

THE next morning, the lawn was wet from an early light rain, and the wall was covered with writing. Mami had seen it when she drove away to work her overtime shift. I saw her mouth twist all up as she looked at it.

I wondered if my name was on the wall X-ed out, but today, only the words *Tres Palmas* were sprayed in two-foot-high writing. No individual gang names—just the name of the group.

It was early on Saturday morning, not even 8:00 a.m., but I called Spooky's house. I had thought about doing it, ever since I had found Albert's phone number in my old notebook from La Vista. I didn't know if it would help or hurt, but I didn't know what else to do. Painting over the graffiti was only getting me into more trouble. I needed a new plan.

A woman answered. I asked to speak to Albert. When she put down the phone, I thought about hanging up, but I didn't.

"Albert, it's Paulo. Remember me from school?"

"Yeah."

"I need you to give a message to Spooky."

"My brother? I don't talk to him much," Albert said. "Sometimes I don't see him."

"If you do see him, just tell him Paulo says, 'Let's chill.' Okay?"

Albert repeated the message back. "You want me to tell him you chillin'?"

"Yeah, exactly that."

When I hung up the phone, I realized I was dripping with sweat. Would Spooky let me get off with that—a bit of an apology?

Now I needed to paint the wall again. Maybe this would be the last time I'd ever have to do it. If Spooky accepted the truce, then things would be cool again. It was possible. Brown Brothers had had a truce with Cactus Posse for more than a year after the police got both sides together in a meeting at the community center.

I got the paint that Manuel had given me from his carport.

I had stopped counting how many times I'd had to repaint the wall. Nikka sat beside me and rested while I started rolling over the graffiti with the new paint. I was absorbed in my work and didn't notice the car slowly rolling down the street until Nikka barked. It was a thumper car, a gray Honda, all lowered and slick, but no music was playing. The car was close, so close that I could see Spooky and Loco inside the car with someone older driving. It looked like No Name.

The car came faster, heading straight for us. I dropped the roller and scrambled behind the wall. I heard a crash and a yelp and then voices from the car yelling. They had smashed their car against the wall. Loco got out and pushed on the front where the crushed fender caught the tire. He pulled, and the tire was free. He leaped back into the car, and No Name reversed it and pulled away with a squeal and smoke piling up behind him.

Then I saw Nikka crumpled against the wall, her nose to the brick.

"Nikka, Nikka!" I called. Nikka didn't move. I bent over and rolled her slightly. I felt a wetness. Blood.

Blood on my fingertips.

"Nikka, Nikka, are you okay?"

Nikka remained limp and motionless. I ran my fingers along her muzzle, checking her mouth and nose for breath. Nothing. Nothing. Nothing.

Nikka was dead.

FIFTEEN

I buried Nikka by the wall. The dirt was soft from the spring rain. I was just finishing covering Nikka with dirt when Mami drove up coming home from work.

Mami walked to me and looked at the dirt and at the shovel in my hands. "What are you doing, Paulo?"

I pointed to the grave. I could only say "Nikka" before Mami had her arms around me and my face was buried in her shoulder.

Later I told her how Nikka was killed. I told her about New Frontiers and Spooky and Loco. Mami's face was white and scared at first, but then she grabbed the newspaper. Her hands were shaking, and she was thumbing through the pages and muttering to herself.

"Here, here we are. Apartments for rent."

She had the classified section out. She began calling numbers for apartment rentals.

"But what about your chickens, Mami? And your vegetable garden?"

Paulo's Wall

"We don't need chickens, and we can buy our vegetables," Mami said in between calls. "I'll give the chickens to Antonio Garcia."

On Sunday, Mami found a two-bedroom apartment for the same price as our house. "It has a pool there, m'ijo, and it's close to the big shopping center. It's in a nice neighborhood," she said. "It's in a different school district entirely. You'll go to another high school. You're not going back to New Frontiers where those boys are. You'll have a fresh start."

The next day I started to pack my clothes, but looking outside the window, I saw the graffiti still on the wall, right above where Nikka was. I went to the garage and got out the last of the paint. I took the roller brush and pan and painted over the graffiti.

As I painted, Mr. Hernandez, who sold bananas and oranges and flowers from a cart that he pushed down the street, stopped to see what I was doing. I showed him Nikka's grave.

Mr. Hernandez knelt down and dug a small hole with his hands. Then he patted a clump of flowers in the spot. "Purple verbena—for Nikka," he said.

Somehow seeing the flowers on the grave calmed me. "Thanks, Mr. Hernandez."

I went inside, and the house seemed quieter

than usual. Mami had wanted to stay home with me today, but she couldn't miss work. They had an important order to fill by Friday, she had explained, her eyes wide and shiny.

Edgar was going to come by on his lunch break to check on me, Mami said. Before . . . when Nikka was alive . . . I would have been angry that Mami was having me checked on like I was a little kid. Now it was crazy, but I didn't mind.

I pulled the grocery list off the refrigerator and took the money from the jar where Mami kept it. I almost picked up Nikka's leash, but then I remembered that I would be walking to the store alone.

At the grocery store, I saw Isabel. I tried to avoid her line, but hers was the only checkout open.

"How's Nikka?" she said, her usual greeting.

I swung the gallon of milk onto the checkout stand.

"How's Nikka?" she said a bit louder, smiling her usual white-toothed smile, her eyebrows moving up almost to her hairline.

Still I couldn't answer.

"Remember, if you ever want to sell that dog . . ." she began and then waited for my usual answer.

I fumbled with the money. As I walked away,

I realized that I had left one bag of groceries behind. I turned, and there was Isabel. She had followed me, carrying my last bag.

Her eyes checked the rack where I always tied Nikka.

"She's gone?"

I nodded, taking the bag from her.

"I'm sorry. I'm really sorry," Isabel said. She moved to put her hand on my shoulder, but I turned quickly.

I didn't want to look at the wall when I reached home, but I couldn't help noticing that next to Mr. Hernandez's verbena, someone had planted a gardenia with pink blossoms.

Edgar brought me a deluxe burrito from Señor Campos, my favorite restaurant. He couldn't stay long because it was his lunch hour, and he didn't ask if I was okay or say anything to make it look like he was checking on me. He just handed me my food and talked about how Señor Campos made the best Mexican food in Los Angeles County and how soft drinks in a can, not from a fountain, were better-tasting. It was pretty cool that he wasn't acting like my baby-sitter.

When he was leaving, he asked me to walk out to his car with him. He reached in the window and pulled out a pot with white flowers—carnations.

He looked a little embarrassed. "For Nikka's spot," he said, motioning to the flowers that marked her grave.

"Thanks," I said. I was beginning to understand why Mami liked him. He wasn't too bad.

The next morning, I found purple and white vincas, a yellow pansy, and several clumps of daisies by the wall. Mami told me the names. She had learned many of them from working at the warehouse. She also had a book with colored pictures that helped her identify them.

In three days, the front of the wall was lined by all kinds of flowers. On top of the wall I placed all the bouquets of cut flowers people had brought.

It seemed as if the entire neighborhood had heard about Nikka. Isabel had told the other checkers from the market that Nikka was gone. They had brought over a flat of flowers from the market and planted them.

That week, Heriberto planted red carnations by the wall. Mr. Sanchez brought orange poppies. Someone from three streets over whom I had never met planted fuchsias, and a woman who worked at the appliance store brought tulips over and placed them by the wall.

Even Yvette sent flowers over, a huge bunch of pink and white knot weeds. She had written a note too.

Dear Paulo,
I'm really sorry about Nikka. Your mom told my mom about it. I know a little bit about what you're going through. I've had trouble at my school with some girls. I hope things get better for you.
Love, Yvette

That was the first note I'd ever gotten from her. Actually, it was the first note I'd ever gotten from any girl. I put her note in my junk drawer. It wasn't really junk in that drawer; it was just a place where I put important stuff I didn't want to lose but didn't know where else to put.

I wondered if Mami had felt this way about any notes my father had written to her. Lately I'd been sitting in the dining room, just staring at my father's photograph. I thought about this guy, Edgar, and my mother. She liked him, and somehow that made my father seem like an ordinary guy. Which he wasn't.

I planted Yvette's flowers right at the center of the wall. It was hard to make them fit, there were so many flowers now.

I had never before seen some of the flowers people brought—brilliant purple cranesbill, magenta dahlias, yellow and red columbine, purple tube-shaped vetch, funnel-shaped gentians, blue harebell, delicate meadow beauties, black-spotted yellow lilies, soft pink bindweed, and sky-blue asters.

A news reporter heard about the wall and came to talk to me. At first I didn't want to talk to her. But she showed me a picture of her own dog and told me smart things her dog could do like hold an egg in his mouth without breaking it, so I relaxed and started talking.

I didn't realize until later how much of the story I had told her. She asked just the right questions with such a sympathetic voice that I told her about the graffiti, the guys from New Frontiers, and, finally, how Nikka had died.

"Why didn't you ever go to the police about these problems?" she asked.

I thought back to the car accident we had seen at Yvette's quincenera where no one had talked to the cop about the drivers fighting. I remembered what had happened in the park bathroom when Nikka had bitten the gangster's leg.

"We just don't do that" was all I could say.

The reporter took a photograph of me

standing by the wall covered with flowers. Later, she came back and gave me a pot of dandelions mixed with yellow daffodils.

"These are for your wall," she said. "I'm really sorry about Nikka. Thanks for the interview."

Manuel called me the next afternoon. "Have you seen the newspaper? You're in it. You're on the front page."

"I am? What does it say?" I asked. I had never been in a newspaper article before. Manuel read it to me over the phone.

It was Paulo's wall, but the gang members didn't care. To them, the tall white wall was a place to show their colors, to tag and claim the neighborhood for their territory.

For 14-year-old Paulo Gomez, the wall now marks the grave of his beloved dog, Nikka, killed by the gang members in a fight over the graffiti.

Gomez lives in the house behind the wall. When he discovered graffiti on the wall, he painted over it, and that angered gang members.

"I didn't want to dis them or take them on or anything. It was just my wall, my neighborhood, and their graffiti made it ugly," explained Gomez, formerly a 9th-grade student at La Vista High School.

Gomez didn't realize he was taking on the gang when he painted the wall. He was harassed at school by gang members and took a knife to school for protection, he said. He was then expelled and sent to New Frontiers.

La Vista Assistant Principal Hilda Porter said, "We can't comment on individual student disciplinary matters, but I can say Paulo was a good student here. I was not aware of any gang problems the boy was having."

Gomez was confronted by three of the gang members last Saturday. His dog, Nikka, was killed when she was hit by a car that the members were driving.

Neighborhood residents have brought flowers to the wall. Heriberto Gonzalez said, "Everyone knew Paulo and Nikka. He is a nice kid, always friendly, never a troublemaker, and he would walk his dog around the neighborhood every day. It's a shame these gang members are hurting everyone."

Now the wall is a blaze of color from

all the flowers the neighbors have planted.

Gonzalez said the wall has brought the neighborhood together. "We're going to form a neighborhood watch group, and we're going to stop the graffiti. We're not going to let Paulo fight this battle alone anymore," he said.

"That's it," Manuel said. "But there's a big color picture of you standing next to the wall, and there are flowers everywhere. It's really beautiful."

"I wish you could see the wall, Manuel. It is pretty. Everyone around here has brought flowers."

"Have you seen the Tres Palmas homeboys?"

"No, not since Saturday. But we're moving at the end of this week. So it won't matter anymore."

"You're moving? Where?"

"Into an apartment on Wemmick Road. It's nice, like yours. We have a pool."

"But what about your backyard?"

"We don't need a backyard anymore, since Nikka's gone."

SIXTEEN

HERIBERTO brought over a copy of the article for me.

"For you," he said.

"Thanks."

"Sorry about Nikka."

"Me too."

"Reporter came."

"Yeah, I know."

"Talked a lot."

"Yeah, never knew you could talk so much."

"Me too."

Heriberto laughed, and I laughed too. It felt good to use those muscles again, to feel my face lighten up.

I made a box of Nikka's things—her leash, her toys, her brush, and her dog shampoo. I couldn't decide what to do with it all. It didn't seem right to throw it away, but I didn't need to carry it to our new place.

"Maybe I'll leave it in the garage for the people who move in after we leave. They might have a dog," I told my mother.

Before Mami could answer, the telephone rang. It was probably Edgar, I figured. He was calling every day now. Mami went to get it, and I started packing my comic book collection. When I looked up again, Mami was standing in the doorway with a smile on her face.

"What did Edgar have to say?"

"That wasn't Edgar," Mami said. "That was your assistant principal, m'ijo, at La Vista. She said she read the article about you in the newspaper and that she was going to look at your expulsion papers and have the school board reconsider your case. They might allow you to go back to La Vista."

"Yeah, but we're moving."

"That's what I told her. She said she'd write a letter to the principal at your new school explaining the situation so you wouldn't have a bad report in your file."

I shrugged. I didn't care about any bad report. If the teachers didn't like me at the new place, that wouldn't matter. I was just going to mind my own business, anyway. I'd go to school, do my work, and come home. I had learned my lesson.

The next day I had almost everything in my bedroom packed. I had found some boxes in the dumpster behind Bargain Barn, and Mami had brought a few from her work.

I was in the kitchen wrapping the breakable dishes when Mrs. Estrada knocked on our door. She handed me more flowers. "Hi, Paulo. These are for Nikka. I know you're feeling sad and probably don't even want to think about it, but you can have the pick of Osa's litter. Any puppy—first choice."

I felt my chest burning. Nikka had liked Concha and Osa so much.

"No, but thank you anyway. My mother and I are moving. We're going to an apartment. With a pool."

"Oh, I'm so sorry. We'll miss you." Mrs. Estrada's face looked sad, honestly sad. She had known me since I was a little boy. Most of the neighbors had known my mother for years. Would they be sad, too, that we were moving?

After I closed the door, I threw myself onto the couch. I thought back to the time when I had asked Mami if we could move to another neighborhood. Nikka had been alive then. I had wanted to get away from this place, from these neighbors. But these neighbors were friends— Heriberto, Mr. Sanchez, the Estradas, Antonio Garcia, even Isabel.

Here we had a yard and a garage. In less than two years, when I was 16, I was going to restore a '50s Chevy. Tío Miguel had promised to help me fix it if I could save enough money to buy one. Heriberto had a Chevy in his backyard that he told me I could buy for $1,000. Nothing on it worked, but Heriberto said with a lot of hard work, it could be fixed.

Most of the people in the neighborhood had lived here for at least 20 years. I didn't know any other house. In the front yard of this house, I had taken my first steps one month after my first birthday. Mami told me how proud Papi had been as I stepped down the driveway.

I had sat on the porch of this house with my mother and father and watched the fireworks from York Field on the Fourth of July. In this house we had sung *villancicos* every Christmas Eve as Mami made tamales. And it was in this house that Papi had coughed blood in the sink, before we knew about his cancer.

It was in this house that I had made my mother cry with happiness when I bought her $60 pearl earrings with money I had saved all year selling my lunch tickets to kids at school. It was in this house that I had trained Nikka, just a puppy, to scratch at the door when she needed to go out.

I hated changing schools too. This new school would be my third one in six months. I missed La Vista. I missed Manuel, Ben Rodriguez, Mr. Hilbert, Mr. Shagallini, even my English teacher, Mrs. Cavanough.

I missed Papi, and, most of all, I missed Nikka.

I went to the window and looked at the wall. My wall. Nikka's wall. Then I went to my bedroom and started to unpack. When my mother got home that evening, I would tell her we shouldn't move. I would be okay. I would be careful. I wouldn't do anything to antagonize the gang.

SEVENTEEN

I went to the wall to plant the gardenias Mrs. Estrada had given me. I had to search for a spot of free soil. The flowers bloomed in a wild array of colors—purples next to reds, oranges mixed with blues and pinks. The flowers made an amazing mix of color. No wonder people stopped and stared at the wall.

People hadn't stopped bringing flowers. Piles of bouquets lined the top of the wall. And the bottom was a mass of flowers, some with notes and cards from people I didn't know. The notes all said nice things like "Rest in peace, Nikka." One person put a card with a photograph of his dog that had died a couple of years ago. The guy wrote, "Paulo, I know how you feel. My dog, Sammy, was my best friend."

Mrs. Estrada said people were driving a mile or two out of their way just to see the wall. She had friends from Lupe's Restaurant who had heard about my wall and had driven from Montebello just to see it. Another newspaper from the San Gabriel Valley had seen the article in the local paper and had reprinted it with the photograph. That made more people drive out to see the wall.

It made me feel good that people liked the wall. Antonio Garcia said we should all plant flowers in our yards. Mama had smiled when he said that. "What a lot a little color can do," she said.

I was busy planting and didn't notice that someone was approaching until it was too late.

It was Spooky.

I scrambled to my feet. Nikka wasn't there to show her teeth and growl. I had nothing to defend myself with except a small shovel. It'd be no match for any weapon Spooky had.

But Spooky didn't want to fight. He had flowers wrapped in cellophane, and he tossed them next to the other flowers.

"Sorry about your dog. We were just trying to scare you, but my homeboy . . . he hit the gas too much," Spooky said, looking at the ground and not at my face. "I have a dog too. I got him when I was a kid. It ain't cool to . . . I mean, sometimes a dog is the only one you can really talk to, you know what I mean? My brother, Albert, he says you're cool. We didn't know. I wouldn't dis a homeboy of Albert's."

I stared at Spooky's shaven head, at the stubble growing where he had shaved all his dark hair off. I wanted to say so much to him. I had too much to say, but all I could get out was, "Don't tag my wall."

"No, I won't." Spooky rubbed a swollen tattoo on the side of his neck. It look raw and painful. "I'll tell my homeboys not to. Cool?"

"You tell Loco to leave the wall alone."

"I'll tell him. Loco's cool. He won't dis you no more."

"Okay."

Spooky walked away, and I sank down on the ground. I picked up the flowers Spooky had brought, thought about throwing them in the trash, and then placed them back on Nikka's grave. I sat by Nikka, by our wall, until it was dark and I had to go inside.

Tomorrow, I would go to Mrs. Estrada's and look at her puppies. Nikka would want it that way.